TEDDY JO

and the Ragged Beggars

TEDDY JO

AND THE
Ragged Beggars

HILDA STAHL

WindRider BOOKS

Tyndale House Publishers, Inc., Wheaton, Illinois

Dedicated with love
to all the school children who listen and learn
as I talk to them about writing!

Teddy Jo Series
 1 Teddy Jo and the Terrible Secret
 2 Teddy Jo and the Yellow Room Mystery
 3 Teddy Jo and the Stolen Ring
 4 Teddy Jo and the Strangers in the Pink House
 5 Teddy Jo and the Strange Medallion
 6 Teddy Jo and the Wild Dog
 7 Teddy Jo and the Abandoned House
 8 Teddy Jo and the Ragged Beggars
 9 Teddy Jo and the Kidnapped Heir
10 Teddy Jo and the Great Dive
11 Teddy Jo and the Magic Quill
12 Teddy Jo and the Broken Locket Mystery
13 Teddy Jo and the Missing Portrait
14 Teddy Jo and the Missing Family

Cover illustration by Gail Owens

Juvenile trade paper edition

Library of Congress Catalog Card Number 89-51918
ISBN 0-8423-6980-5
Copyright © 1982 by Hilda Stahl
Printed in the United States of America

95 94 93 92 91 90 89
 8 7 6 5 4 3 2 1

Contents

1. Ragged Beggar

Teddy Jo looked longingly back at Happy as he barked and waved his long bushy tail. The morning sun was already hot on her dark head and she knew she had to hurry or she'd be late for her first day of special reading at summer school.

A boy rode past on a ten-speed. A robin flew from the soft grass and landed in a maple tree. Teddy Jo clenched her small fists and pressed her lips tightly closed to hold back the angry scream that rose inside her. How could Mom and Dad sign her up for summer school and not tell her until the day before? Summer was not for going to school! Summer was for playing and working with Grandpa and having more time for art.

Would she be the oldest one taking special reading? Maybe no one would guess that she was almost thirteen years old. She was short and small for her age. At nine, Paul was almost as tall. He thought he was so big! She knew he was sitting at home right now watching TV and laughing at her because she couldn't read fifth-grade level reading even though she was going into seventh grade in September.

"You are going, Teddy Jo," Dad had said this morning before he and Mom went to work in Grand Rapids. "You must improve your reading."

She had bitten her tongue to keep back the sharp retort. Now that Dad was a Christian he'd taken almost too much interest in her. Before, he'd never noticed or cared what she did.

"You'll be thankful for special reading classes once school starts again," Mom had said.

"I don't want to go!"

"Theodora Josephine!" Mom had said in her warning voice. "You are going, and you'll be on time!"

So, she was going and she would be on time. She glanced at her watch. She'd make sure she got there exactly on time, not a minute or even a second early. Her jeans felt hot against her thin legs. Her yellow tee shirt was tucked in neatly the way Linda had insisted. And her long brown hair was brushed and clipped back with yellow barrettes.

"Mrs. Frazer, Bill's mother, works at the school," Linda had said with her hands on her slender waist. "And I will not let you go to school looking ragged or dirty. I don't want Mrs. Frazer or Bill to think my sister is a slob."

Teddy Jo kicked a rock and it skittered down the sidewalk ahead of her. Linda was so picky! So what if she didn't look like she'd just stepped out of the pages of *Seventeen*? Teddy Jo wrinkled her straight nose. *She* didn't care at all, but Linda did. Linda stayed in the bathroom for hours brushing her long, dark hair, putting on makeup, and just staring at herself to make sure she was gorgeous and would make the boys notice her.

Teddy Jo stopped at the curb and waited for several cars to pass. How could she endure three long weeks of summer school? Every morning for the next three weeks, she'd have to sit inside and read! Oh, it was too terrible to think about!

Just as she crossed the street someone darted behind a tree, then looked furtively around. It was a dirty-faced girl with blonde curls and ragged clothes. A police car turned onto Oak Street and the girl dove behind lilac bushes and waited until the car was out of sight.

Teddy Jo stopped and looked down at the girl. She looked up with frightened brown eyes. "Are you in trouble?" asked Teddy Jo in a low voice.

The girl swallowed hard as she stood up. She was taller and slightly heavier than Teddy Jo. "I might be."

"You're new in Middle Lake, aren't you?"

The girl nodded.

"I'm Teddy Jo Miller."

The girl hesitated. "I'm Carlie . . . Smith." She looked around quickly, then held out her dirty hand. "Do you have a dollar I can have? I'm hungry and I haven't eaten for two days. My mom and dad don't have work and there are five of us kids and we need money for food." She sounded as if she'd burst into tears any minute.

Teddy Jo looked at Carlie's ragged clothes and her thin dirty face and felt sorry for her. "I only have fifty cents."

"I'll take it," Carlie said quickly.

Teddy Jo dug it out of her jeans and held it out. Carlie grabbed the two quarters and pushed them into her pocket, then turned and ran to Washington Street and disappeared from sight.

A car stopped beside her and Teddy Jo turned with a startled gasp. A police officer stuck his head out the window.

"Did you see a young girl in ragged clothes run past here?"

Teddy Jo hesitated, then nodded. "Did she do something wrong?"

The man frowned. "She's begging. There's a law against that and I want to warn her." He shook his head and drove away.

Teddy Jo held her breath, then let it out in a sigh as she saw the patrol car turn left instead of right on Washington. Carlie was safe for a while.

Teddy Jo glanced at her watch and made a face. If she didn't have to go to school, she'd find Carlie and warn her against begging. Maybe she could find a way to help Carlie and her needy family.

"Oh, why do I have to go to school?"

How she wanted to run after Carlie, but instead she ran toward the school. Her tennis shoes slapped against the sidewalk. Suddenly she stopped. Standing at the corner of the school was Carlie Smith! How had she gotten here this fast?

Teddy Jo shot a look around for the police car. It wasn't in sight. She ran to Carlie and gripped her arm.

"Get your hands off me!"

Teddy Jo stumbled back. "You're not Carlie!"

"I didn't say I was."

She stared at the boy who looked like Carlie. He had the same blond curls and ragged clothes. He looked the same age.

He frowned at her. "What're you staring at? Didn't you ever see a beggar before?"

His sharp words and gruff manner angered her. She lifted her chin. "I've seen a beggar before and I saw the policeman who was chasing her!"

The boy's face turned as white as the fluffy clouds in the summer sky. "Did he catch her?"

"Maybe."

He groaned.

Teddy Jo cleared her throat. "No. He didn't catch her. She ran and he didn't see where she went, but I did, and I know her name."

"No, you don't!"

"It's Carlie Smith!"

"Shh!" He darted a look around, then gripped Teddy Jo's arm. "I don't want you saying anything about this to anyone! I don't want anyone to know who we are!"

"I suppose you're her brother."

"Her twin. I'm Heath." He pushed his face

close to hers and his breath was warm against her. "Don't tell what you saw or who we are!"

A shiver ran down her spine. She backed away, then broke into a run. She hit the school door and pushed it open with a rush. The cool air enveloped her and she ducked into the first hallway and sucked in her breath. Her blue eyes closed into slits and she wrapped her arms around herself. She hoped she'd never see those ragged beggars again.

2. Grandma and Grandpa

Teddy Jo walked slowly along the dirt road to Grandpa's behind Paul and Linda. Happy stayed close to Paul's side. Occasionally the afternoon sun slipped behind a cloud, making the weather perfect for walking the two miles to Grandpa's.

Linda looked back and frowned. She knew Teddy Jo was still upset because of school. She should be thankful for the chance to learn to read better. Linda walked faster with her head held high. She was tall and slender. Her long legs were tanned a golden brown. Today she'd braided her hair in one long French braid down her back. It showed off her high cheekbones and wide blue eyes. Her shirt and shorts were the same shade of blue as her eyes. She knotted her fists. How could she and Teddy Jo be in the same family? Wouldn't Teddy Jo ever grow up and notice life around her? It had helped when she'd become a Christian three years ago. She didn't throw temper tantrums or hit people or swear the way she used to. And she cared for others. She was always trying to help someone in need. Linda bit her bottom lip thoughtfully. Being a Christian really had made a difference in Teddy Jo. Would it make a difference in her? Would it take away the lonely feeling inside? Linda walked faster. She would not think about that! Her family was always talking to her about God and his love and she didn't want to dwell on that when she had lots of other things to think about.

Teddy Jo looked across the ditch to the grove of trees. A movement among the trees caught her attention. She stopped, her heart racing. Carlie Smith looked out at her, then ducked out of sight. Why would Carlie be out in the country? Was she still hiding from the police?

At Grandpa's Teddy Jo followed Linda and Paul through the back door of the two-story house where Mom had lived until she'd married and left home. The aromas of toast and bacon made Teddy Jo's stomach tighten with hunger. One peanut butter and jelly sandwich had not filled her. Her mouth watered just thinking about a bacon, lettuce, and tomato sandwich on toast with a tall glass of cold milk.

"Hi, Grandma," said Linda with a wide smile.

Grandma hugged Linda, then turned to hug Paul and Teddy Jo. She smelled like lily-of-the-valley.

"Where's Grandpa?" asked Teddy Jo. She looked around the kitchen. It looked almost the same as it had before Grandpa had married Anna Sloan. Now, they had a microwave oven because Grandma said it made cooking quicker and easier and left her with plenty of time to write her books, which she was famous for.

"Ed's working in his woodshop," said Grandma. "He has to finish a cradle for Mrs. Brooster's granddaughter by tomorrow."

Linda watched Grandma as she talked to Paul and Teddy Jo. Linda sat with her elbows on the table and her chin in her hands. When she was as old as Grandma, she wanted to be just as pretty. Grandma knew all about the right makeup and clothes. It was fun to sit and talk to her. Today she'd promised to help Linda with a new hairstyle. She moved restlessly. Why didn't Teddy Jo and Paul run to find Grandpa so she could be alone with Grandma?

Paul looked around questioningly. "Where's Honey, Grandma?"

"We made a pen and doghouse for her in the backyard next to Queen. She and Queen are finally friends."

Paul hit the door at a run to see the big collie and little cocker spaniel. Happy jumped up from where he rested beside the back door and ran beside Paul to the pen.

Teddy Jo caught the screen door before it banged shut and closed it quietly. Birds sang in the trees surrounding the house. Paul's voice rang out as he greeted the dogs.

Just inside the garage Teddy Jo stopped and

watched Grandpa gluing the spindles on the cradle. He filled the garage with his presence. He was dressed in a matching tan shirt and pants. He turned and a smile lit up his rugged face. "Hi, Grandpa." Her heart almost burst with love for him. Once she'd hated him, hated staying with him when Mom and Dad were separated and thinking of divorce. Finally she'd learned to love him and love God as her heavenly Father.

"Hello, Teddy Jo. You're looking very pretty today."

She flushed and looked down at her dusty shoes. He was the only person who ever said she was pretty.

"How did school go today?"

She caught his arm and gripped his large hand. "It was awful, Grandpa! I hate to read, I'll never, never learn to read!"

He caught her by the arms and looked down into her upturned face. "Teddy Jo, you'll never learn to read as long as you say that you can't. God created us so that our words affect us. Our words create. Your words build a mental block against reading. You know that God made you in his image. You have his ability. If you start talking in a positive way, your mental block against reading will collapse and you'll learn."

He had never lied to her before and she knew he wasn't now. She knew what he was saying was in the Bible. He'd shown her before, but she kept forgetting. She bit her lip and hung her head.

He drew her close and she could smell the

18

aroma of wood shavings and stain that was always a part of him.

"Teddy Jo, I love you and I want what is best for you. You can learn to read well! I know it! I want you to know it and start saying it. Will you do that?"

She nodded into his neck.

He held her out from himself and smiled down at her. "Say after me, 'I have God's ability in me.'"

"I have God's ability in me."

"I can learn to read."

"I can learn to read." She swallowed hard.

"Soon I will be the best reader in the entire class."

Her heart leaped at the thought. "Soon I will be the best reader in the entire class!"

Grandpa hugged her close again with a happy laugh. "That's right. God will help you learn, Teddy Jo. Your part is to stop saying words that defeat you and start saying that you can read well and are learning every day to read better. Practice reading and make the most of summer school."

That made her think of Carlie and Heath Smith. Quickly she told Grandpa about them and he frowned thoughtfully.

"I think we should try to find them and see if we can help them," he said with a shake of his gray head.

She thought of Heath's anger and she shrugged. "Maybe they won't want help."

"If two kids go around town begging, they

need help." Grandpa scratched his head and tugged at his open collar. "We'll see what we can do."

"I don't know where they live."

"I'll ask around." Grandpa picked up the spindle and put it in place. "I hate to think of a family starving when we could give them help."

She nodded. Grandpa had taught her to be kind and loving to others but sometimes she forgot, especially when that someone was as grouchy as Heath.

"Did you see what I have out in the shed, Teddy Jo?"

"No." She looked eagerly toward the open door.

"Let's go look." Grandpa laughed as he caught her hand and walked into the bright summer day. "I found it in the ditch in front of the house yesterday afternoon."

"Is it a bird?" She knew he'd taken care of sick and hurt birds until they could fly away again.

"Nope."

"A deer?" White tail deer lived around them and often he took care of them.

"Not a deer. You're way off."

Teddy Jo opened the shed door and walked inside. She could smell dog food and grain that was stored there for the dogs and Smokey.

Grandpa stopped beside a box and Teddy Jo looked in to find a large cat with long gray hair. It looked up with a meow.

Teddy Jo touched the soft hair and the cat purred. "What's wrong with it, Grandpa?"

"His foot is hurt and he has a deep cut right here." Grandpa pointed to the cut near the back leg. "By the time he's well, we should be able to find his owner."

"How do you know he wasn't just dumped?"

"He's too friendly and secure with people. He came from a family that loved and cared for him."

Teddy Jo rubbed the gray hair. "Maybe we'll find a notice in the paper." She knew people often put notices in the paper when a pet was missing. "Or someone will call you and ask if you've seen it."

Grandpa nodded. Everyone in Middle Lake and the surrounding area knew that Ed Korman took care of animals, then found homes for them if they were strays or found their owners if they belonged to someone.

"Don't worry, kitty, we'll find your home," said Teddy Jo softly. "Grandpa and I will."

3. Trespassing

Linda stepped carefully around the tangled wild blackberry bushes and stopped under a gigantic oak. She fanned her damp face with her hand. A squirrel chattered from the top of a nearby tree. A deer whistled, then leaped away, crashing through the underbrush. A deerfly landed in Linda's hair, buzzing. Linda slapped it away with a shudder. Why hadn't she stayed on the road instead of cutting through the woods? Teddy Jo and Paul loved the woods with the bugs and wild animals and tangled underbrush. Linda was sure she didn't understand why!

Why should she want to look at Roger Peck's deserted house? She hadn't heard from him in several months. He was probably still in Detroit and she'd never see him again. Tears stung her eyes. She had loved him once and maybe she still did—a little.

She stepped around a clump of bushes and stopped dead, her eyes wide in surprise. Just two feet away stood a tall blond boy a few years older than she. He wore faded jeans and a sleeveless tee shirt that showed off his strong arms. His brown eyes were narrowed in anger.

"You are trespassing!" He stepped toward her and her legs trembled, almost collapsing under her slight weight.

"I didn't know." She swallowed hard. "I thought I was on Peck property."

"You're not!"

She looked around with a frown. "Am I lost?"

The boy's frown disappeared and he studied her with interest. She was pretty and he didn't think she was out to make trouble. "You aren't lost. This property did belong to the Pecks, but our family bought it and now we live here. I'm Mick Yeager."

She smiled. "I'm Linda Miller. I live in town, but my grandpa lives just a short way from here. Are you still in high school?"

"I'll be a senior. You?"

"Sophomore." She wanted to tell him she was a senior, but she knew he'd find out the truth and she'd be caught in a lie. Oh, why couldn't she be older? Why hadn't she allowed Grandma to cut and curl her hair the way she'd suggested?

"Who's your grandpa?"

"Ed Korman."

Mike frowned thoughtfully. "I don't think I know him. We're too new to the area to know many people." He looked over her shoulder and around her. "Are you alone?"

"Yes. I left my sister and brother with Grandpa and Grandma and I came for a walk by myself. I really am sorry for trespassing."

"That's all right. I shouldn't have jumped on you for it. Come to the house and meet my family."

She hesitated, then fell into step beside him.

"I was looking for my little sister's lost cat. It's going to take us time to get used to country living." Mick held a branch aside and let her pass. He liked this girl and he wanted to find a way to keep her around for a while so they could get acquainted.

Linda's heart skipped a beat. Mick seemed to be a very nice boy and she wanted to get to know him better. There was something different about him. He wasn't at all like the boys she dated.

"We moved here from Battle Creek." A twig caught in Mick's curly hair and he pulled it out and dropped it to the ground. The smell of pine hung heavy in the air from the stand of pine trees to their left. "My dad worked at Kellogg's, but he wanted to get back to the country. He and Mom both were raised on farms, so they're loving it here. It's taking the rest of us a little longer to get used to it."

"I know what you mean. I hated it when my family moved to Middle Lake. It's such a small town! Someday I'm going to have an apartment of my own in Grand Rapids."

Mick stopped just inside the clearing and looked at the old farmhouse and the outbuildings.

He flushed painfully. Why had he brought Linda here? Now, she'd know what a run-down farm they had. He cleared his throat. "This is home. That's my dad working on the tractor. And my mom over there in the garden. She said she didn't care if it was too late in the season, she's still going to grow a garden. Joy's inside taking a nap. She's four. The twins are sitting on the back steps, probably plotting something as usual. And I have one more brother, but I don't see him right now. He's ten and he never sits still."

Oh, how well she knew what he meant! "I have a brother who is nine. The only time he sits still is when he's watching TV and even then you have to practically nail him down." She laughed and he liked the sound of it. "I have a sister who is almost thirteen, but we won't talk about her." She closed her mouth with a snap. Why had she said that? He didn't want to hear about Teddy Jo.

"Come on. I'll introduce you to my family." He touched her arm, then quickly dropped his hand and stuffed it into his pocket. He'd never had a girl friend and it made him feel funny to walk beside such a beautiful girl. Would she know that he was shy with girls? Maybe she was shy with boys.

They stopped beside the tractor. The man turned and pulled his cap off and his light brown curls clung damply to his well shaped head. He smiled and his white teeth flashed. "Hello."

"Dad, this is Linda Miller. Linda, my dad, Ely Yeager."

"Hi," said Linda with a smile.

Ely pulled off his work glove, wiped his hand down his jeans and held it out to Linda. She clasped it and his large hand closed around hers firmly.

"You're our first visitor," Ely said in his deep voice. "Welcome. Mick, why don't you take her inside for a glass of apple juice?"

Mick felt the flush start deep inside and he fought against it. He hated it when his neck and face and ears turned red. "We'll say hi to Mom first," he said, forcing himself not to mumble.

As they walked across the yard toward the garden plot Linda said, "I like your dad."

"Thanks. I do, too." Mick laughed and shook his head. Wouldn't he ever learn how to talk to a girl? He stopped and his mother pushed herself up and dusted off her jeans. "Bess Yeager, Linda Miller."

"Hi, Linda. Welcome to our home."

"Thank you, Mrs. Yeager."

"We're going inside to get a drink," said Mick. "Is there any apple juice left?"

"Yes, unless the twins drank it all." Bess pushed back her blonde curls and her dark eyes twinkled. "Sometimes I think the twins inhale the contents of the refrigerator. This country living has increased their appetites."

Suddenly a boy dashed from behind the shed and gave a loud yell. He didn't stop, but disappeared from sight around the house. Bess laughed and shook her head. "That's Ty. He's pretending to fight aliens, any aliens he thinks of at the time. He always wins."

"Maybe I could bring my brother Paul over sometime to play with him." Linda looked at Mick as she said it and she saw the glad light in his eyes. It warmed her down to her toes.

"We'd be glad to have him," said Bess. "Come any time. We're always home."

Mick walked toward the steps where the twins sat watching him. If they said one thing to tease him, he'd make them very sorry! "Linda, this is Carlie and Heath, the twins."

"Hi," they said together. Carlie looked at Mick with a sly smile and Heath rolled his eyes.

Mick waited until Linda spoke to the twins, then pushed past them into the kitchen. He was glad that it was clean and tidy. "Have a chair. I'll get us some juice." He opened the refrigerator. "Or would you rather have water or milk?"

"Apple juice is fine. I am thirsty from walking through the woods." She sat down thankfully and crossed her bare legs and dangled her foot. She felt right at home in the cheery yellow kitchen. She took the glass of cold juice thankfully and sipped it.

Mick sat down across the table from her and drank his juice. He tried to relax, but he couldn't think of anything to say. She probably thought he was a big jerk.

"The school bus will pick you up at the end of your drive at about seven-thirty each morning and drop you off about four," Linda said.

28

"How do you know?"

"I knew the boy who lived here."

"Oh." He wanted to ask how well she'd known him, but he couldn't force the words out. "Do you walk to school?"

"Yes. We live about four blocks from the high school. Sometimes I catch a ride with friends." She rubbed the condensation off the outside of her glass. "Do you play football?"

"I did. I don't know if I'll have time this year. I'm getting a part-time job, maybe signing up for co-op if your school has it."

"We do. I know some who have part-time jobs and they like them."

Just then a small girl ran into the kitchen, a teddy bear clutched in her arms. Her face was red from sleep and her eyes wide with questions. "Did you find Gray, Mickie?"

"Come here, Joy." He pulled her onto his lap and held her close. "I looked and looked for Gray, but I couldn't find him. But I found Linda. Say hello to Linda." He smiled at Linda. "This is Joy."

"Hi, Linda." Joy turned back to Mick. "You said we'd find Gray. You said God would help us when we prayed."

"He will help us find Gray, Joy. Our heavenly Father always hears and always answers. We'll find Gray."

Linda sat very still, her blue eyes wide. Mick was a Christian! What was she getting herself into this time?

29

4. The Yeager Family

Mick sat on a fallen log with his elbows on his legs and his chin in his hands. A fly buzzed around his blond curls but he didn't notice it. He frowned and groaned low in his throat. How could he have let Linda Miller walk away without getting her phone number or address? He'd said he'd call her, that he'd see her again. That had been two days ago. The phone book had about twenty Millers listed. He couldn't just start calling until he found the right one!

Mick lifted his head and narrowed his brown eyes thoughtfully. Linda had said her grandpa lived nearby. What did she say his name was? He slammed his fist into his palm. How could he be so dumb? A beautiful girl had walked into his life and he'd let her walk right out again with a polite good-bye and a love-sick smile. Would she be waiting for his call? Or had she forgotten about him entirely? Maybe, maybe she'd walk in the

31

woods again and he'd find her and talk to her and learn her phone number and address.

He looped his thumbs in his pockets and slowly walked along the narrow deer trail toward his house. "Heavenly Father, I know that you care about me. Help me to find a way to get to know Linda Miller. And help me not to be shy around her. You're helping Joy find her cat, now help me find Linda." Mick laughed softly. "Thank you, Father, for not thinking that I'm stupid. I love you and I always want to please you."

He stepped into the clearing just as the twins walked out of the back door of the house. He called to them, but they were deep in conversation and didn't hear him. With narrowed eyes he watched as they walked down the driveway toward the dirt road. What were they plotting this time?

Carlie kicked a stone into the tall weeds of the ditch. "I only got five dollars in three days, Heath. That's not going to help out at all."

Heath brushed a fly away from his blond curls. "It's better than nothing, Carlie. I got four dollars and together that's nine. We can help buy groceries with it."

Carlie stopped and squinted against the sun as she looked at her twin. "Are you sure we're poor?"

"Dad had to sell our dirt bikes just to pay a bill, didn't he? That's poor!"

Carlie sighed as she blinked back hot tears. "Why didn't we stay in Battle Creek? We had money and everything! I guess I like it here, but I don't want Mom and Dad to have to worry about paying bills."

Heath nodded grimly. "We'll have to work harder! And not get caught. You watch to make sure the police don't see you begging, Carlie. We're too young to get jobs, but we can help this way."

Carlie walked slowly along the dirt road. The sun turned her curls a shiny gold. Frogs and peepers sang from the creek that ran through the property next to them. "We can't even find a paper route! You have to drive a car to have one here, instead of a bike like we did at home." She wrinkled her pert nose. "Home? This is home now! How are we going to make friends?" She thought of Teddy Jo Miller. She couldn't be friends with Teddy Jo. She knew about the begging.

"Maybe Mom and Dad will get tired of country living and move back to Battle Creek," said Heath as he kicked a clump of dirt. It sprayed across the road and spattered against the weeds. "I will never find a club here to belong to!"

Carlie caught his arm. "Hey, why don't we start one ourselves? We could give it a name and everything!"

"Are you kidding? I want a club without girls!"

"So? Ours can be different. We can start a club with both boys and girls and we can do helpful things just like the club you belonged to." Her brown eyes sparkled. "We could call it the King's Kids!"

Heath laughed. "That's good, Carlie." Sometimes she really did have good ideas. "And we'll get to know the kids in our church and maybe they'll want to join it."

Carlie's face fell. "What if they find out about us begging? What if they find out that we're poor? That would be just awful!" Her voice ended in a loud wail.

Heath doubled his fists. "We'll have to be more careful. That's all. We'll have to disguise ourselves with more than just ragged clothes. Once our garden comes up and we have food from that, we can quit begging. Then we'll start the club. Maybe."

"Oh, it would be terrible if Mom and Dad found out what we've been doing!" Just then she saw Ty peeking at them from behind a tree beside the road. Her stomach tightened. Had he heard them? He was always playing games and spying on whoever was around. "What are you doing, Ty?"

"Just playing," he called back. He ducked out of sight and laughed softly as he leaned against a tree. One of these days he'd get close enough to hear what the twins were planning. He knew about the ragged clothes and the dirt smeared all over them, but he couldn't find out what they were doing.

Slowly he crept through the trees toward the house. He peeked out and saw Dad walking toward the tractor. Ty ran toward him with a loud whoop.

Ely looked up with a laugh. "I've never seen such a change in one little boy."

"What change?" asked Ty as he danced around Dad.

"In the city you were quiet and watched TV too much. Now, you spend your whole day outdoors, running around and playing and helping when I need you."

Ty stopped and grinned up at Dad. "I like living in the country. I'm going to be a farmer when I grow up."

"How would you like to learn to drive the tractor?"

Ty's brown eyes widened. "It's so big!"

"I learned to drive when I was about seven or eight and by the time I was ten I could plow and disc by myself."

Ty shook his head. "I'm ten and I never rode on a tractor before we moved here. I want to learn to drive one. Will I need a driver's license?" He knew that Mick had taken driver's training when he was sixteen and had gotten his license. Ty couldn't wait for that day!

"You don't need a license to drive a tractor. You need to learn how and then practice until you can do it well." Ely boosted Ty onto the tractor seat and Ty looked way down at the ground and shivered with excitement.

Ely started the tractor and the noise shut off all other sounds. Ty felt the vibrations throughout his body and he laughed happily. Someday he'd go back to Battle Creek and tell all his old friends that he knew how to drive a tractor.

He saw his mom and little sister walk out of the house and he waved and shouted. He knew they couldn't hear him over the noise.

Ely shifted the gear and the tractor jerked and moved forward. Ty held tightly to Dad.

Joy watched the tractor until they drove around the barn into the field. She tugged Mom's hand. "We have to find Gray. He must be hungry. He misses me and he wants to see me."

Bess nodded. She knelt in front of Joy and wrapped her arms around her. "Honey, we'll find Gray."

Joy held her little hands around her mouth. "Gray! Come, Gray!"

Bess tugged her pink tee shirt over her darker pink shorts. "We'll walk around for a few minutes and look for Gray and call him, then we have to work in the garden."

"Will my flower seeds be growing out of the ground yet?" asked Joy as she looked up at Mom with wide brown eyes.

"Not yet. We have to wait more days, but one of these days we'll walk to the garden and we'll see all kinds of plants poking their little heads out."

"And we'll pick the vegetables and eat them and pick the flowers and put them in vases on the table. Right?"

Bess laughed. "Right."

Joy watched a bee fly past and land on a wild flower at the side of the shed. She ran to the flower and watched, then ran back to Mom and walked around the shed and the house and the barn, calling for Gray.

Tears filled Joy's eyes and ran down her round cheeks. She knuckled them away and sniffed. "I want my kitty so bad! I want God to answer right now and send my kitty to me!"

"Honey, God is watching over Gray. We'll find him." Bess hugged Joy tightly. "We have to work in the garden now and pull out those nasty weeds that try to take it over."

"We hate weeds, don't we, Mom?"

"We sure do! Weeds choke out our good plants and make our garden look bad."

The back door slammed and Mick walked out with the car keys dangling in his suntanned hand. "I'm ready to go, Mom. See you later."

"Did you get the grocery list, Mick?"

"Yes, Mom. And the money for them. I think I'll check at the grocery store to see if they could use a stock boy or carry-out boy. I'd like to have a job the rest of the summer."

"I saw an ad in the hardware store for a clerk. You could ask there, too, Mick." Bess shielded her eyes against the sun as she looked up to talk to Mick. He was several inches taller than she. "We'll see you later."

"Bring me a surprise, Mick," said Joy as she caught his hand and squeezed it.

He laughed and tickled her neck. "Why should I bring you a surprise?"

"Because I want one and you love me."

Mick and Bess laughed and Joy looked at them, wondering why they were laughing.

Mick slipped into the car and slowly drove out of the drive. Maybe he'd see Linda in town. His heart leaped. If he did, he would not be shy and tongue-tied! He would walk right up to her and speak to her and ask for her phone number and address. Perspiration dotted his upper lip. "I will not be afraid to talk to her! No, I won't!"

5. Lost
in the Woods

Joy stopped abruptly and looked up at the tall
trees. Her heart stopped, then raced in panic.
How had she walked this far into the woods
without knowing it? Mommy had said never to
walk into the woods alone, not even to look for
Gray. Oh, why had she forgotten? What was she
going to do now?

Tears filled her eyes and blurred her vision as
she looked around. "Mommy! Mommy, come
find me!" Her voice shook and she swallowed
hard and called again.

A dog barked in the distance and Joy shivered
and plucked at her sunsuit. An ugly scratch ran
from her dimpled knee down the side of her leg
to the top of her white sock. "I'm lost," she
whispered weakly.

At the house Bess looked in the girls' bedroom
for Joy and frowned. "Where is Joy?" She hurried
through the house, calling Joy without an answer.

Just outside the back door of the house Bess shielded her dark eyes against the sun and looked all around. "Joy! Where are you? I want you, Joy!" Bess's stomach tightened with fear. There were so many things that could happen to a little girl alone. "Oh, Father in heaven, watch over my little girl! Send angels to protect her and bring her home safely!"

Bess ran to the barn, calling Joy. She wanted to run into the woods and search for her, but if Joy walked to the house and found no one at home, she'd be terrified. She could easily be just out of hearing, and would come walking to the house any minute.

Bess groaned. Mick was still in town, Ely and Ty were on the tractor on the other side of the trees and the twins were gone wandering as usual. Why didn't someone come home and help her look for Joy?

"Father, Joy is in your care." Tears ran down Bess's face as she prayed.

On the outskirts of Middle Lake Teddy Jo and Paul walked slowly along the dirt road that led to Grandpa's. Happy ran ahead, barking at every insect or animal he saw.

"Let's walk through the woods today," Teddy Jo said suddenly. "It's too hot on the road."

"Maybe we'll see a deer." Paul ran down into the ditch and up on the other side. "Happy! Come here, Happy! We're going through the woods!"

Happy barked as he ran back to Paul and

Teddy Jo. Burrs caught in Happy's white, tan, and gold hair. He zig-zagged along the deer trail with his nose to the ground. Squirrels scolded from high in the trees.

Teddy Jo stopped to pick a few wild flowers to take to Grandma. The smell irritated her nose and she held them away from herself.

Paul's stomach grumbled with hunger and he smiled thinking about the chocolate chip cookies that he knew Grandma had made. She'd told him on the phone that she'd finally finished her book and was taking time out to do some baking. This was the perfect day to visit Grandma and Grandpa. Paul grinned. Any day was a perfect day to visit them. Something exciting was always going on at their house. At home he had to listen to Linda talking on the phone to boys and Teddy Jo complaining that Linda never helped with the housework.

Teddy Jo walked around a large oak and looked up at a black walnut tree. It reminded her of the acres of black walnut trees at Grandpa's place. His grandpa had planted black walnut trees for his future and Grandpa had continued the tradition. He had sold some of the trees to a furniture company for veneer and bought a house in Middle Lake for the Miller family. Teddy Jo smiled. She had her own yellow and white bedroom and didn't have to share it with Linda. They had money enough to pay their bills and buy groceries now. Once they'd lived in cheap apartments and run-down houses and Mom and

41

Dad had fought all the time. They were Christians now because Grandpa had helped them to see and know God's love. Teddy Jo thought life would be almost perfect if she didn't have to go to summer school and learn to read better. She wrinkled her nose. Grandpa had said that she could learn because she had God's ability in her. He had said to watch what she said and to say that she *could* read and that she *was* learning to read better. She sighed as she pulled free of a tangled raspberry bush that caught at her jeans and tee shirt.

Suddenly Teddy Jo stopped and lifted her head, listening intently. Paul saw her and stopped, his heart racing. What had she heard?

Teddy Jo gripped Paul's arm. "Do you hear a little kid crying?" she whispered. What would a little kid be doing in the woods?

Paul listened and he heard the sobbing sound from deeper in the woods. "Maybe it's a wild animal in pain," he whispered, his face white and his blue eyes wide.

"Let's find out what it is." Teddy Jo took a hesitant step forward. Her legs trembled, but she forced them to walk. The sound grew louder and she knew it was a child sobbing. Was someone lost in the woods?

Joy knuckled her tears away and tried to stop crying, but she couldn't. Her heart raced in fear as she heard something walking toward her. Was it a wild animal that would eat her for dinner? She wanted to run, but she couldn't move. She stood between two large oaks with one fist at her side and the other rubbing her eye. Her yellow and pink sunsuit was torn and dirty and bits of dirt, leaves, and twigs were caught in her blonde curls.

Teddy Jo saw her and stopped in surprise. She hadn't really believed she'd find a lost child. Happy dashed forward with a loud bark and the little girl screamed a loud, piercing scream that hurt Paul's ears.

"Down, Happy!" called Teddy Jo as she ran to pull the dog away from Joy.

Paul caught Happy's collar and held him back. "Who is she, Teddy Jo?"

"I don't know, Paul." Teddy Jo caught the girl's arms and held her. "Stop screaming! You're all right now! Our dog won't hurt you and neither will we."

Joy swallowed hard as she stared up at the girl with tangled brown hair and bright blue eyes. Fresh tears welled up inside Joy and streamed down her dirty face. She wanted to ask the girl to take her home, but she couldn't speak.

"What's your name, little girl?" asked Teddy Jo softly.

Joy sobbed harder.

"Where do you live? Are you lost?" Teddy Jo stood helplessly in front of the girl. "Tell me your name and where you live and I'll take you home."

Joy wanted to tell her, but she couldn't stop crying and she couldn't talk.

Paul swallowed hard. He was going to start

crying in a minute if he watched the little girl any longer. "Let's take her to Grandpa's. Maybe he'll know who she is. Grandpa knows everything."

"Good idea," said Teddy Jo. She caught the little girl's small hand in hers. "We'll get you home. Don't worry. Come with us and we'll find your mom and your dad."

Joy sniffed hard and obediently walked with Teddy Jo and Paul.

At Grandpa's Linda stood at the living room window and watched Teddy Jo and Paul walk down the drive. Linda gasped. Why did they have little Joy Yeager with them? Were the other Yeager children close behind? Linda's heart leaped. Maybe she'd see Mick today. Maybe he'd been too busy to call her or come see her.

She ran out the front door and stopped beside Teddy Jo. "Where did you pick up Joy?"

Teddy Jo stared at Linda in surprise. "Do you know this little girl?"

"Sure. She's Joy Yeager."

"We found her lost in the woods," said Paul. He was glad that they could finally get the little girl out of the woods so she'd stop crying. He'd never seen so many tears in all of his life.

Linda knelt before Joy and wiped her face with the tail of her tee shirt. "Do you remember me, Joy? I'm Linda. I know your brother Mick."

Joy's tears stopped and she nodded. "I want my mommy," she whispered brokenly.

"I know you do," said Linda softly. She slipped her arms around Joy and pulled her close.

44

Teddy Jo's mouth dropped open and she blinked in surprise. She'd never seen Linda do anything so nice.

"What's going on here?" asked Grandpa.

Teddy Jo smiled at him as she slipped her hand through his arm and rested her head against his strong arm. He smelled like sawdust and paint. "We walked through the woods and found this little girl. Linda says her name is Joy Yeager. Linda knows where she lives."

Linda looked up with a nod. "The Yeagers bought the Peck's place. They haven't lived there very long."

Joy looked familiar to Teddy Jo and she wrinkled her brow in deep thought. Did she know someone named Yeager? She couldn't remember and the harder she tried, the farther back in her memory it fled.

"I'll get the car and we'll take this little girl home," said Grandpa, squeezing Joy's plump shoulder.

"I want to go home," said Joy in a tiny voice. She gripped Linda's hand and wouldn't let go.

"We'll take you now," said Linda with a pleased smile. Maybe Mick would be home and they could talk again.

6. Glad Homecoming

Mick held his mother close and pressed his cheek against her soft hair. "We'll find Joy, Mom. Stop crying. I'm home and I'll go after her. I waved Dad in and he'll be here soon with Ty. We'll find Joy. Don't worry!" His stomach tightened painfully. They had to find Joy! It would be terrible if she fell into the lake on state land behind their property or walked through a bog. No! He couldn't think that way! His trust was in God and God loved them. He was protecting little Joy wherever she was.

Bess wiped her tears and stood straight. "I'm all right now, Mick. It was terrible being here alone and not able to find Joy."

"I know, Mom."

The noise of the tractor filled the air and then was suddenly cut off. Ely and Ty leaped down and ran to Bess and Mick.

"What's up?" asked Ely as he saw the strained

look on his wife's face. "I saw you wave to me before, but I didn't think you wanted me until Mick waved me in."

"It's Joy, Ely. She's lost!" Bess wrapped her arms around Ely and pressed tightly against him. "Oh, Ely!"

"Shh, Bess. It'll be all right. God hasn't let us down yet, has he? He won't now." Ely kissed her, then looked up as a car drove in.

Mick turned. His heart leaped as he recognized Linda Miller sitting in the front seat. Had she come to see him to find out why he hadn't called her?

Bess spotted the little blonde head and she cried out with gladness as she ran to the car. "Joy! Oh, you found my baby!"

Linda stood beside the car and watched the Yeager family hug and kiss Joy. A great yearning welled up inside Linda. It would be wonderful to love Teddy Jo and Paul as much as Mick loved his little sister.

Finally Ely stepped back. "Thank you, Linda, for bringing Joy back to us."

"My sister and brother found her in the woods," said Linda, motioning toward them standing with Grandpa beside the car. "This is Teddy Jo, Paul, and our grandpa, Ed Korman."

Grandpa shook hands with Ely, then with Bess and Mick. "I'm glad to meet you folks. You're making something of this place and I'm pleased to see it."

Ty and Paul looked each other over carefully.

Teddy Jo nudged Paul. "Go talk to him," she said under her breath just for Paul's ears.

Paul flushed and stepped forward. "Hi. I'm Paul Miller."

"I'm Ty Yeager. My name's really Tyrone, but everyone calls me Ty. Want to look around our place?"

Paul nodded. He hadn't been there since Roger Peck moved away.

Teddy Jo watched them run toward the barn. As she turned back to listen to Grandpa she saw a boy and girl her age walk up the driveway. She stared at them with narrowed, thoughtful eyes. Did she know them? She bit back a gasp. They were the ragged beggars!

"Hi, Mom," said Carlie with a smile. She looked around and her face turned chalky white when she saw Teddy Jo. Oh, what if Teddy Jo said something about seeing her before in town?

"Carlie, Heath, this is Teddy Jo Miller and her grandpa, Ed Korman," said Ely. "You've already met Linda. And the boy with Ty is Paul."

"They brought Joy back," said Bess, hugging the little girl tightly. "She was lost and they found her and brought her back to us."

"I think we could use a glass of lemonade, Bess," said Ely. "How about it, Mr. Korman?"

"Call me Ed." He nodded. "I'd enjoy a glass of cold lemonade."

"Don't go in, Teddy Jo," whispered Carlie in panic. "We want to talk to you."

Teddy Jo hesitated, then nodded. She did want

to hear what the twins had to say. And Carlie had said her name was Smith!

"Linda and I are going for a walk," said Mick before he lost his courage. He looked at Linda with his brow raised questioningly and she nodded. Relief washed over him, but he didn't let it show. God had answered and brought Linda to him. He would not waste time by being shy!

Joy clung to her mother's hand as they walked to the house. Suddenly Joy stopped and pulled free. She ran back to Linda and threw her arms around her. "Thank you for bringing me home. I love you!"

Linda gasped. Her face turned a bright red as she stared in surprise at the little girl clinging to her. Finally she squeezed Joy's shoulder. "I'm glad I could help you, Joy."

Joy pulled away and ran to her mother and disappeared inside the house. She was tired and hungry.

Linda blinked back tears as she turned away from the house and looked toward the road.

"She's some little girl, isn't she?" Mick's voice was soft and full of understanding.

Linda nodded, but still couldn't speak.

Mick touched her back and nudged her forward and they walked side by side away from the twins and Teddy Jo. At the end of the driveway he turned left and they walked slowly along the dirt road that led back to state property.

"I wanted to call you, Linda." He forced back

the flush that threatened to turn his face and ears red.

She glanced up, her eyes bright. "You did?"

"I forgot to get your phone number. Do you know that there are twenty Millers in the phone book?"

Linda laughed breathlessly. "There are?"

Mick laughed and she liked the sound of it. "I thought about starting at the first one and going down the line, but I didn't."

"Dad's name is Larry. You wouldn't have had to go very far."

"I'm glad you came today. I prayed that the Lord would help me find you. And he did!"

Linda's heart jumped a funny little jump. Had God really answered or was it a coincidence that she was here with Mick right now?

"I asked about a job at the grocery store today."

"What did they say?"

Mick shrugged. "They don't need anyone right now, but they said they'd keep me in mind. Do you have a job?"

"I baby-sit sometimes, but that's all." She bit her bottom lip as she kept her eyes on the ground ahead. "Someday I want to be a model." Would he laugh and say it was too big a dream for her?

"You're beautiful enough to be a model."

Her eyes sparkled as she lifted them to his. "Do you really think so?" Other boys had said that, but somehow she knew that Mick wouldn't say it unless he really meant it.

He nodded, but couldn't say any more about her looks without blushing. "I haven't decided what I want to do after high school. If I go to college, I'll have to work myself through. But I could do it."

"I'll bet you could do anything that you set out to do."

Her words warmed him and he found the courage to reach for her hand and hold it as they walked and talked.

Back at the house Teddy Jo tapped her foot and waited for an explanation from the twins. "I want to know why you said your name was Smith instead of Yeager!"

"It's none of your business," snapped Heath with a scowl.

"Don't, Heath," said Carlie, nudging him. "She could've told right off, but she didn't. We can trust her."

Teddy Jo's curiosity was stronger than her anger. "What do you mean, trust me?"

Heath jabbed Carlie. "You talk too much!" He didn't want Teddy Jo to know anything. If she found out how poor they were, she might tell everyone around. It would be embarrassing when school started to have everyone look at him and say he was poor.

Carlie could tell that Heath meant business. She didn't dare tell Teddy Jo why they were begging. "Heath and I are out scouting around for kids to be in our club, Teddy Jo."

Heath relaxed and leaned against the grill of the car.

"What kind of club?"

Carlie locked her fingers together behind her back. "We want to start a club for both boys and girls, one that we can have fun in and help people in need. Heath and I were trying to get money to start the club." The lie stuck in her throat. She knew as a Christian that it was a sin to lie, but it was out and she couldn't take it back.

"We'd call the club the King's Kids," said Heath. He squirmed restlessly. How could they lie with one breath and talk about being a King's Kid with the next?

"It's a club for Christians," said Carlie, trying not to blush.

"I'm a Christian!" said Teddy Jo excitedly. "I'd like to belong to the club."

"Great," said Carlie, forcing her voice to sound enthusiastic. "We could help people in need." She almost choked on that. Who was in more need than they? "We'd help old people do their yard work or get groceries and all kinds of things."

"I think that's a great idea," said Teddy Jo. Why hadn't she thought of that? She knew lots of girls that would enjoy a club like that. "When do we start it? I have a little money saved that can help out."

Heath walked away, his hands in his pockets, his shoulders hunched. Carlie glared after him. How could he leave her alone at a time like this?

She managed to smile at Teddy Jo. "I don't know when we'll start. We'll let you know."

"You won't have to go around begging for money now," said Teddy Jo.

"No! No, we won't," said Carlie quickly. "We decided that this would be our last day to beg." A great sadness filled her. She'd asked Jesus into her life when she was only six years old and never before had she told lies. Oh, but she was bad! What if Jesus wouldn't forgive her?

Teddy Jo nodded. "I'm glad, Carlie."

Inside the barn Paul and Ty stood looking across the yard. "We found our horse Smokey right in that shed," said Paul, pointing. "Roger Peck tied him in there and told someone to feed and water him until he got back. The boy never came and one day me and Teddy Jo were looking around and we heard a noise in the shed. It was Smokey and his ribs showed and everything."

"Did he die?" asked Ty with a shudder. He loved animals and he wanted a horse of his own.

"He looked like he would, but Grandpa knows how to take care of sick animals. He took care of Smokey and now he's healthy and strong and we ride him a lot. You can come to Grandpa's sometime and ride with us if you want."

"I'd like that."

Paul did, too. He and Ty were going to be good friends. And if Ty never found out that he wet the bed sometimes, they'd stay good friends. "Hey, want to hear how we found our dog?"

Ty nodded excitedly.

Paul told him about the wild collie, Queen, and her pups. "Dad shot Queen because she was wild and he thought she'd scare away deer, but me and Teddy Joy were so sad that he took Queen to a vet and the vet made her well. Now, Grandpa has Queen for his own. While she was wild she had pups and me and Teddy Jo found them. Grandpa gave all of them away except for Happy. Dad said we could have Happy. So, that's how we got our dog."

"We have a cat," said Ty. "But I want a dog. If you find another dog, tell me and I'll take him. We could take our dogs for walks together and everything." He looked across the yard at the twins and Paul's sister. "We can all be friends."

Just then Paul saw Linda walk into the yard with Mick. They were holding hands. He giggled under his breath and his thin shoulders shook. "I guess it does look like we'll all be friends."

7. The Beggar Comes Again

Teddy Jo looked longingly out the schoolroom window. The morning rain had stopped and the sun shone brightly, making the raindrops sparkle like millions of beautiful diamonds. Why, oh, why was she stuck inside on such a glorious day? She glanced down at her reading workbook. How could she continue to complain after she'd promised the Lord that she'd really try to learn to read and be happy about it? God wanted his best for her and she knew his best right now was for her to be a good reader.

"Sorry, God," she muttered under her breath.

She set her jaw stubbornly and picked up her pencil. She would finish her workbook now! When it was time to read aloud, she'd do that. The morning would pass just as the last few mornings had passed and soon she could be outdoors playing soccer. Later she'd work on her painting.

A fly buzzed at the window. Music drifted in from down the hall. Meagan York sneezed, then giggled in the silence.

Mrs. Bloom called Teddy Jo to her desk and Teddy Jo jumped right up with her book in her hand. Never again would she hang back and say she wasn't ready. A smile tugged at her lips when she saw the surprised look on Mrs. Bloom's round face. And when Teddy Jo made only three mistakes Mrs. Bloom patted her hand.

"You did very well today, Teddy Jo. Keep up the good work."

"I will!" And she meant it, too. She'd bite her tongue hard before she'd allow herself to complain about class or before she'd say that she would never learn. She would learn! Someday she'd be the best reader in her grade! Her heart leaped and she smiled as she walked out of school into the bright sunny day.

She stopped on the sidewalk in front of the school and breathed deeply. Her stomach growled with hunger. At home she'd make a tuna and lettuce sandwich with a glass of milk. If Paul hadn't already eaten all the ice cream, she'd have a bowl of French vanilla with chocolate topping. Her mouth watered just thinking about it.

Two girls waved from across the street and Teddy Jo waved back as she ran down the sidewalk toward Oak Street. Just ahead she saw a ragged beggar knocking at Mr. Petersen's door. Teddy Jo stopped and doubled her fists and pressed her lips tightly together. Carlie and Heath had said they wouldn't beg again after she'd given them her money yesterday. How dare they!

Carlie looked over her shoulder and spotted Teddy Jo. The door opened and Mr. Petersen said, "Can I help you?"

Carlie flushed and shook her head, then dashed across the yard. She leaped over a flower bed and ran as fast as she could to get away from Teddy Jo. The six dollars that she'd already collected seemed to burn a hole in Carlie's ragged pants. Oh, why had Teddy Jo Miller walked down that street just at that time?

Carlie's feet touched the soft grass of the park and she ran faster, dodged behind a hedge, and dropped to the ground, gasping for breath. A twig stabbed into her leg and she pulled it away and tossed it toward a flower bed with yellow marigolds in bloom.

Pigeons landed nearby and pecked at the ground, cooing softly. Boys and girls shouted as they played soccer on the other side of the swings and slides.

Carlie pulled her floppy hat off her hot head and fanned her sweaty face. Why had they ever left Battle Creek? Why had she ever met Teddy Jo Miller? No one else had taken an interest in her enough to ask her name. Sunday in church she'd met several girls and although they were nice, they hadn't been very friendly. Right now she didn't need friends. She wanted to be left alone to help her family the only way she could.

She licked her dry lips and rubbed her parched

throat. Just as soon as she could breathe normally again, she'd get a drink from the fountain. With her knees pulled to her chin she looked across the park at a small girl on a swing being pushed by her mother. Carlie smiled. One of these days she'd bring Joy to the park to play. Joy would love it!

At a sound beside her Carlie looked up. She gasped and leaped up. How had Teddy Jo found her? "What do you want, Teddy Jo?" Carlie asked sharply as she stood with her fists doubled at her sides and her chin thrust forward.

Teddy Jo stepped closer. Her eyes were dark with anger and perspiration dotted her face. "You said you wouldn't beg anymore. You said you had enough money to start the club."

Carlie tossed her head and pretended that she wasn't embarrassed and ashamed. "So what? I was wrong. Heath and I got to figuring the expenses and we saw that we needed more."

"Then get it from the kids who will join the club!" Teddy Jo shook her head and her hair flipped and tumbled around her head and down her slender shoulders. "You don't need a lot of money just to start." Teddy Jo leaned forward and looked Carlie right in the eye. "I think you are begging for money for another reason."

Carlie gasped. Her fingers tightened on the hat brim curled in her hands. "You don't know what you're talking about!" The first time she'd seen Teddy Jo, she'd told her that she was begging because they had no money and no food. What if Teddy Jo believed her?

Teddy Jo tucked her hair behind her ears. She could see that Carlie was agitated. "You tell me why you're begging and maybe I can help you."

"No!" Carlie shook her head and her curls bounced. "I don't need help! I told you we need the money to start the club!"

"You don't have to shout, Carlie *Smith* Yeager! I can hear you. I don't believe you, but I can hear you."

Carlie spun around and ran from Teddy Jo. But Teddy Jo ran after her and caught her arm and jerked her to a stop.

"You don't have to run from me, Carlie. I want to be friends. Can't we be friends? Come to my house with me now." Teddy Jo snapped her mouth closed. Why should she want to be friends with this ragged beggar? But she did and she couldn't help herself.

Carlie's mouth dropped open.

"Will you come to my house now, Carlie? We could eat lunch. I was going to make a tuna sandwich for myself."

Carlie cleared her throat. "I'd like to come, but first I have to change these clothes and clean up." She walked toward the park restroom and Teddy Jo walked with her.

While Carlie went inside to change Teddy Jo sat on the stone bench in the shade of a tall maple. She saw Dara Cook with her brothers near the slide. Teddy Jo waved and Dara ran across the grass to her.

"Hi, Teddy Jo. What're you doing?" Dara flipped back her white-blonde hair. She was dressed in lavender shorts and a white tee shirt with tiny sleeves. A gold heart necklace hung around her slender neck.

"I'm waiting for someone, Dara. I see you're watching your little brothers."

"It's my summer job. Do you have a summer job, Teddy Jo?"

Teddy Jo wrinkled her small nose as she sat on her hands. "I don't, except to help around the house."

Dara sat down and kicked her dangling feet back and forth. "Cathy told me this morning that you go to summer school for reading. That's good, Teddy Jo. Now, you won't be embarrassed to read in front of others."

Teddy Jo started to say something against school and reading, then said instead, "I'm learning to read better every day."

Just then Carlie walked out, looking very different in clean pink shorts and a tee shirt and no dirt on her face and arms. Her curls made a soft halo around her pretty face.

"Carlie, I want you to meet a friend of mine," said Teddy Jo. "Dara Cook, Carlie Yeager."

"Hi, Carlie. I'm glad to meet you. Do you live in town?"

"No. Out in the country near Teddy Jo's

grandpa." Carlie clutched the bag of ragged clothes and tried to act normal.

"We're going to start a club called King's Kids," said Teddy Jo. "It's for Christian kids. We'll do things together for fun and to help others. Would you like to join?"

Carlie stifled a groan. Now, they'd have to really get the club organized.

"I'd like that," said Dara. "I think Cathy Norton would, too."

"Cathy's my neighbor," explained Teddy Jo to Carlie. "She has a brother the age of your brother Ty. Maybe they'd want to play together sometime." Teddy Jo turned to Dara. "We have to go now. I'll see you again and I'll call you to let you know when our first King's Kids meeting is."

Carlie's stomach tightened into a hard knot. Her lie was crashing around her. What would Teddy Jo do if she learned that the club wasn't really going to be, that she had no intention of starting one?

At the Miller home Teddy Jo handed Carlie a tall glass of cold milk. "I'll fix the sandwiches fast."

"I'll help you." Carlie set her glass on the table and pushed her bag under the table out of sight. What if Linda or Paul walked in and saw the ragged clothes inside it?

"You can toast the bread." Teddy Jo drained the water off the tuna and dumped the bits of fish into a glass bowl. She mixed in salad dressing and a few pieces of chopped onion and stirred it together. She dug one finger in it and lifted it out and licked it. Oh, but it tasted delicious!

Carlie held out the toast. "Teddy Jo, you won't tell anyone about me, will you?"

"No, I won't tell anyone. But I'd sure like to! You know it's against the law! If the police catch you, you'll really be in trouble." Teddy Jo began spreading the tuna on the toast. She pulled leaves from the head of lettuce and placed them onto the tuna. She dropped a sandwich onto a saucer and handed it to Carlie. "You don't want the police to catch you and call your parents and tell them what you've been doing, do you?"

Tears sparkled in Carlie's brown eyes and she quickly turned away. "That would be just awful!"

"Then stop begging!"

Carlie whirled around. "I can't! We need the money!"

Teddy Jo sank to her chair. "For what, Carlie?"

Carlie slowly sat down. "For food," she whispered hoarsely. "We don't have money since we moved here. Heath and I wanted to help."

"Oh, Carlie!"

"Promise me you won't tell anyone! Not anyone!"

Teddy Jo nodded. "I promise. But Carlie, don't beg money from others. I'll help you and I know Grandpa will. He always helps people in need."

"You promised not to tell!" cried Carlie in alarm.

"I won't tell. I'll tell Grandpa that I know someone who needs groceries and he'll get them and I'll give them to you." Teddy Jo leaned forward earnestly. "Are you sure your family is too poor to buy groceries?"

Carlie barely nodded.

Teddy Jo sighed heavily. "All right. I'll help you, but you have to promise me that you won't beg again."

Carlie bit her bottom lip. Finally she said, "I promise, Teddy Jo." A great weight lifted off her and she smiled. "I hate to beg. I hate to dress in those ragged clothes! Thank you, Teddy Jo. You are my friend."

Teddy Jo smiled and picked up her sandwich. "Let's eat, shall we?"

8. Picnic

Mick stopped his car outside the Miller's garage. His throat was dry and his palms sweaty. He tugged at the neckline of his tee shirt and rubbed his hands down his jeans. What if Linda had changed her mind about going on a picnic with him?

How did other guys do it? No one else seemed to be this afraid to go with a girl. Most of his friends in Battle Creek had been going with girls for at least two years, some of them longer. They'd all teased him and said he was a late bloomer.

Mom had said, "Enjoy yourself today, Mick. Just relax and be yourself. This should be a fun day, one that you'll always remember." She'd kissed his cheek and patted his arm. "You're a wonderful boy, Mick. Any girl would be proud to be seen with you."

He nodded and slipped out of the car. He would not be nervous! With his head up he walked to the front door.

Happy barked from the side of the house where he was tied to his dog house. The TV played inside the Miller house. Mick's hand shook as he pressed the doorbell.

Teddy Jo peeked out the window and saw Mick Yeager and she sighed and wrinkled her nose. "Linda, he's here!"

In the bathroom Linda turned from the mirror with a glad laugh. "Let him in, Teddy Jo. I'll be right out!"

Teddy Jo reached for the doorknob. "Turn the TV down, Paul."

Paul fell over his feet as he rushed to lower the sound of the Saturday morning cartoons. He could feel the excitement that had been coming from Linda since he got up this morning.

Teddy Jo jerked open the door and stepped aside. "Come on in, Mick. Linda said she'd be right out."

Mick smiled at the somber girl. "You're Teddy Jo, right?"

She nodded.

He didn't know what else to say to her, so he stood just inside the door and waited with one hand clasped around his wrist and his feet apart.

Teddy Jo walked to the front window and stood watch once again. Cathy Norton was coming over to talk about the King's Kids club. She'd probably see Mick and forget about anything else. Teddy Jo frowned. Why didn't Linda hurry so they could leave before Cathy came? Once Cathy started thinking and talking about boys, it was hard to get her mind on important things.

Just then Linda walked into the living room, smelling strongly of perfume. "Hi, Mick." Her heart jumped and she smiled. Her blue eyes sparkled with excitement.

"Hi," said Mick. Had his throat closed over so tight that he couldn't speak without his voice breaking? Linda looked beautiful in her jeans and flowered blouse. He wanted to tell her, but he couldn't force the words out, not with Teddy Jo and Paul listening intently to everything they said.

"The picnic basket is in there," said Linda, motioning toward the kitchen.

He walked with her to the kitchen. He could smell fried chicken. "Did you fry chicken for us?" he asked in surprise.

"Yes. I like it better than hot dogs, don't you?"

"Yes. But frying chicken is a lot of work."

"I didn't mind." She took his arm and he stiffened. "Let's go out the back door, shall we?"

He walked outdoors with the basket in one hand and Linda holding the other. He would not be shy! "Did you bring your swimsuit in case we decide to go swimming, Linda?"

"Yes. Right here." She swung the bag that she carried and laughed. "I'm glad we're going today." She slid onto the front seat of his car and watched him walk around to the driver's side. For some reason she liked Mick better than she'd ever liked her other boyfriends. She'd loved Roger

Peck, but she hadn't liked him very much. She liked Bill Frazer, but not the same as she did Mick. And Mick was a Christian! She frowned. Christian or not, they were going to have fun today!

Mick backed out of the drive and drove down Oak Street toward Main. "What subject are you majoring in in school, Linda?" Would she think he was boring if he talked about school?

She shrugged. "I suppose English. I try not to think about it." She laughed. "What about you?"

"Business. I'm studying computers. I like art, too."

"You do? So does Teddy Jo. She's won awards for her acrylics. We think she's good."

"I'd like to see her work sometime." He couldn't imagine the sober faced girl painting.

They talked most of the way to the lake. Mick felt relaxed and proud of himself for not blushing every time he opened his mouth to talk.

Later they walked slowly along the sandy beach. Warm wind blew Linda's long dark hair away from her. The sand felt warm on her bare feet. Her jeans were rolled up to her calves to keep from getting wet when waves broke over the sand.

Several teenagers ran past, shouting and laughing. A seagull dipped low and flew away with a cry. The sun shone bright in a brilliant blue sky.

"Your grandma and grandpa came over for supper last night."

Linda looked up at Mick in surprise. "They did?" If she'd known, she'd have conveniently been at their house so she could've gone with them.

"They're nice people. I enjoyed your grandpa's stories about the animals he's taken care of." Mick stopped with a laugh as he looked down at Linda. "Guess what? The gray cat he found in his ditch and is nursing back to health is none other than our lost cat, Gray."

"No kidding?"

"Joy is going to be very happy to see Gray." Mick smiled just thinking of the happiness on Joy's face when she learned about Gray. "In fact, Joy's probably at your grandpa's right now to see him. Ed said that in a couple more days Gray will be as good as new."

Linda bit her lower lip. "Do you . . . do you think God answered your prayer, or was it a coincidence?"

"I believe God answered." Mick nodded his head. "I thought it was wonderful that God chose your grandpa to take care of Gray."

That kind of talk made Linda feel very uneasy. She'd never talked about God or anything religious on a date. "I think we should eat now, don't you? I'm hungry." She wasn't very hungry, but she had to think of something to get Mick off the subject of God. She heard enough about God and Jesus at home.

"Fried chicken sounds good to me right now." Mick walked in silence for a while. "Linda, I know there are people who think that answers to prayer are coincidences and I think that's sad. They miss out on seeing miracles happen."

"Oh?" So much for getting off the subject.

"Miracles happen all the time around us, but we have to have our eyes open to them." He stopped again and smiled down at her. "It was a miracle that you came back to our place. I had forgotten to get your phone number or address. I prayed that just as God was helping Joy to find Gray, he would help me to find you. You drove right into our yard and got out of the car and it made me very happy. It was a miracle from God and not a coincidence. It was an answer to my prayer."

Tears stung her eyes and she ducked her head.

"Isn't it wonderful to know that God loves us that much?" Mick walked on with Linda close beside him. He wouldn't tell her that it was a miracle that he could open his mouth and talk to her.

Later they sat at the picnic table, drinking the last of their Pepsis and enjoying each other.

"The food was delicious, Linda, but I think you made too much."

She groaned softly. "I think I ate too much, but it did taste good, didn't it?" She looked across the table at him and couldn't look away.

"Next time I'll bring the lunch. I'll put some steak and potatoes together in foil to cook on the grill."

She smiled, glad that he was planning on a next time. She wanted it, too, much to her surprise. He was very different from the boys she'd dated. She hadn't had to fight him off or urge him on. Just being together seemed enough.

Mick leaned forward with his elbows on the worn table. "How long have you been a Christian, Linda?"

She gulped and her face turned as white as the paper plates they'd eaten on. "Why do you ask?" Her voice shook and she cleared her throat.

"I just wondered. I want to know everything about you."

"How long have you been a Christian?"

"Since I was ten. I can remember my dad praying with me. I had heard all my life that God loved me and sent Jesus to die in my place, but all at once I realized that God loved *me* and sent Jesus to the cross for *me!* I wanted to give him myself. And I want to help others know Christ."

She clenched and unclenched her hands in her lap. "What would you say if I told you that I'm not a Christian?"

He stared at her, wondering if she was teasing him for some strange reason. But he could see she was serious.

Abruptly she jumped up. "Don't just sit there in shock! Say something!"

Slowly he walked to her side. "You're a wonderful girl, Linda."

She lifted her chin defensively. "But?"

"But nothing. One of these days you'll know in your heart that God loves you, and then you'll make him part of your life."

Her blue eyes flashed. "No! Don't talk that way! I'd like to go home now." She started to throw things into the basket but he caught her hands and held them firmly. Finally she lifted her face to him.

"It's all right, Linda."

She burst into tears and he slowly pulled her against his strong chest. He held her without speaking, but silently prayed for her. After a few minutes she pulled away with a watery smile.

"Do you hate me, Mick?"

"Never!"

"Do you mind if we go home? I'm suddenly very tired."

"Linda, that empty feeling that you have felt inside yourself can only be filled with God. That deep yearning you have is for him."

She shook her head. "I don't want to talk about it."

He picked up the picnic basket and walked her to the car.

9. Broken Promise

Teddy Jo stuffed the grocery list into her pocket with the money that Linda had given her. She sighed loudly and looked around at the green lawns and multicolored flowers in bloom. Today was so boring.

"Boring?" She stopped in her tracks and shook her head. What was she thinking? Was she becoming like Cathy or Dara who thought every day was boring, unless of course a boy talked to them or they talked about boys?

"I am not bored!" she whispered firmly. But what was that strange feeling inside her? She wasn't hungry. Just a few minutes ago she'd eaten two peanut butter and jelly sandwiches, five cookies, and a glass of milk. No, she wasn't hungry. She frowned thoughtfully as she walked around a toy truck in the middle of the sidewalk. What was the strange longing inside her? Impatiently she forced her mind off it and thought about how well she'd done in reading again today.

Soon she'd be able to read fifth grade reading without any problem, and after that sixth and finally seventh.

She smiled and lifted her head proudly. Nobody would make fun of her reading before long, not even Marsha Wyman. Sometimes Marsha was nice to her and sometimes she wasn't.

Teddy Jo stopped at the curb and waited for a pickup to pass. She ran across the street and then slowed to a walk. The sun warmed her.

Maybe she should invite Marsha Wyman to join King's Kids.

She gasped and shook her head. How could she do that? Marsha wasn't a Christian. She went to church often with her grandma, but that didn't make her a Christian.

Just then Teddy Jo saw someone slip behind a tree that stood in front of the City Bank. It was Carlie dressed as a beggar again! Teddy Jo narrowed her eyes and pressed her lips tightly together. Carlie had promised not to beg again! How dare she break that promise?

Carlie peeked around the tree just as Teddy Jo ran toward it. In a flash Carlie raced away with Teddy Jo after her. They ran through yards and down an alley. Finally with a burst of speed and a great tackle, Teddy Jo caught Carlie around the legs and they sprawled to the grass at the corner of the vet's office.

Teddy Jo gasped for breath. Her mouth was dry and her face wet with sweat. "You promised not to beg again, Carlie," she gasped out.

"You think you're so smart!"

Teddy Jo's head snapped up and her eyes widened. "Heath!"

He pulled off his floppy hat and fanned his wet face. Damp curls clung to his well-shaped head. His brown eyes were dark with anger. "Can't you ever mind your own business, Teddy Jo Miller?"

Her heart jerked a funny little jerk and she stared wide-eyed at him.

He saw her shock and his heart softened and his anger faded. Carlie had told him what she'd offered to do to help. He smiled slightly. "I hope you didn't get hurt when you tackled me."

She swallowed hard. "I didn't. I hope I didn't hurt you."

"You didn't. I'm pretty tough."

"Me, too."

He laughed softly. "I've noticed."

She flushed, but couldn't look away from him. His eyes were so beautiful! Oh, what was she thinking? With a frown she said brusquely, "I thought you weren't going to beg again. Carlie promised!"

"*I* didn't promise! I wanted to help Dad. He needs a new part for the tractor and I wanted to get money for him to buy it." Why was he explaining it to her? It wasn't her business to know or question what he was doing. But for some strange reason he didn't want her to think badly of him or to dislike him.

"Grandpa might know where you could get a tractor part. He knows everything!"

Heath chuckled. "He does, does he?"

Teddy Jo flushed again and laughed. "Well, he does! We could go talk to him."

"You and I?"

She nodded. She didn't want Heath to leave her and she couldn't understand why. "First I have to pick up a few groceries and then we could go."

Heath looked down at himself. "I think I'd better get out of these clothes, don't you?"

"I would like to see you burn them!" Her blue eyes flashed. "I don't want the police to pick you up!"

He leaned forward, his nose almost touching hers. His breath fanned her face. "Thanks for caring, Teddy Jo."

She couldn't move. Her insides felt all weak and soft and her heart thudded loud enough for everyone in Middle Lake to hear.

"How old are you, Teddy Jo?"

"Almost thirteen," she whispered through dry lips.

"And I'm fourteen. It's perfect." He jumped up and pulled a folded plastic bag from his pocket.

She frowned up at him as he peeled off his ragged clothes and stuffed them in the bag. What was perfect?

"Now I feel better," he said as he rubbed the last of the dirt off his face with a wet washcloth he had put in a plastic bag. His jeans and tan knit shirt were clean and made him look like a different boy.

78

Teddy Jo's breath caught in her throat and she wanted to sit and just look at him.

He held his hand out to her and without hesitation she took it. His hand closed around hers and an excited shiver ran down her spine. He pulled her to her feet and dropped her hand and she wanted to reach out and take his again.

"Where are you going to get groceries?"

"Joe's Market." She glanced at her watch. "We'd better run."

He slung the bag over his shoulder, caught her hand and said, "Let's go!"

She ran beside him and she felt as if she had wings on her heels. Several minutes later she was walking through the store with Heath beside her. She took the groceries to the check-out and then walked out with Heath carrying the groceries for her. She carried his bag of beggar clothing and could still feel the warmth of his hand on the handle of the bag.

"Do you play tennis, Teddy Jo?"

Suddenly she wanted to learn tennis. "No."

"What sports do you like?"

"Soccer." Her eyes sparkled as she said it. "Do you play soccer?"

"Not very well."

She smiled brightly. I could teach you. I'm good at it."

"And I'll teach you tennis. I'm good at that."

"Great!"

"How about tomorrow morning?"

Her heart sank. How could she tell him that

she'd be in school in the morning? Urgently she sought for something to say. "How about the afternoon?"

"Sure. I'll meet you at the park at one."

She felt twenty feet off the ground. "Tennis or soccer?"

"Tennis. I'll bring the rackets and balls." And if Carlie tried to tag along, he'd make Mom keep her home.

As they walked into Teddy Jo's yard, Cathy Norton stepped outdoors. "I've been waiting for you, Teddy Jo. Linda said you'd be right back." Cathy looked from Heath to Teddy Jo in surprise.

Teddy Jo swallowed hard and gripped the bag tighter. "Cathy this is Heath Yeager, Carlie's brother. Cathy lives next door."

"Hi," said Heath with a smile.

"Hi." Cathy sounded breathless. How had Teddy Jo found such a good looking boy to walk with her? Didn't he know Teddy Jo wasn't interested in boys?

"We have to go," said Teddy Jo sharply. She saw the look in Cathy's eye and she wanted to get Heath away from her fast.

"But we were going to do something this afternoon," said Cathy.

"I'll talk to you later, Cathy." Teddy Jo frowned at her and finally Cathy ran across the yard to her house and slammed the door after her.

"We don't have to go see your grandpa," said Heath.

"Yes, we do! He'll know what to do to help your

dad with his tractor." Plus, she wanted to spend more time with Heath. She opened the door and set the groceries just inside the door. No one was in the living room and for once the TV was off. "Linda, here are the groceries! I'm going to Grandpa's."

Linda stepped out of the kitchen. "You can't go alone and you know it." She saw Heath and stopped and a slow smile spread across her face. Teddy Jo with a boy! Miracles really did happen! "Be back by supper."

Teddy Jo ducked out and walked with Heath. She had seen the look on Linda's face, but she didn't want to think about it, nor about why it was so important for her to be with Heath Yeager.

"I'll take my bag now, Teddy Jo." His hand brushed hers as he took the plastic bag and her stomach fluttered strangely.

At Grandpa's Teddy Jo quickly told him what Heath needed and he nodded.

"You came to the right place," Grandpa said with a smile. "Just yesterday a man was here to pick up a chair I fixed for him and he told me about his business. He has tractor parts for old tractors that you can't find anywhere else. I think he'll have what your dad needs, Heath. I'll give him a call and we'll go right over."

"I don't have much money." Heath flushed as he spoke. He was thankful that Teddy Jo hadn't told her grandpa how he'd gotten the money.

"It won't take much," said Grandpa. He turned to Teddy Jo. "You can stay here if you want."

81

"I want to go with you," she said quickly.

"Let's go, then."

Teddy Jo walked between Grandpa and Heath with her head high and her back straight. Happiness bubbled up inside her and she laughed.

10. A Visit to the Library

Teddy Jo walked slowly down the aisle and studied the line of books on the shelves. She heard Grandma and Grandpa the next aisle over, helping Paul choose a book. Grandma had offered to help Teddy Jo, but she'd said she could do it alone.

She stopped at the books on sports. Would anyone tease her if she checked out a book on tennis? She glanced at Linda near the fiction titles.

"I'm glad you're doing something with Heath," Linda had said after Teddy Jo arrived home from playing tennis with Heath. "He's a nice boy."

"I didn't do very well at tennis."

"You'll learn. You're good at sports."

Teddy Jo turned back to the books with a pleased smile. She was good at sports and Heath had said with practice she'd be good at tennis. But it was so hard to remember all the rules! A book would help her. She heard Paul laugh at something Grandpa said and she was glad this library didn't have strict rules about silence. Mrs. Boggs didn't let anyone shout, but she said they could speak in a normal voice. Mrs. Boggs was nice. She probably knew where every book in the whole library was kept, and she'd probably read them all, too.

Teddy Jo spotted a book on soccer and she pulled it out and looked at the pictures. She flipped through the pages, stopping once in a while to study a playing position.

Someone nudged her and she looked up to find Carlie Yeager.

"Hi," said Carlie with a glad smile.

"Hi." Teddy Jo smiled, then looked over Carlie's shoulder to Heath. "Hi."

He smiled, but before he could speak Carlie said, "We came to get books for summer reading. Mom says that we have to read during the summer or we'll forget how by September when school starts."

"Not me," said Heath. "I read all the time. I came to get a book on soccer."

Teddy Jo beamed. "You did?"

He nodded with a laugh that showed off his even, white teeth.

"Not me!" said Carlie with a shrug. "I'm going to get a book that's easy to read." She walked off with her bouncy step toward the children's section where Ty and Paul stood talking together.

Dust particles danced in the sunlight that

streamed through the tall windows. Two adults that Teddy Jo didn't know stopped to talk to Grandma and Grandpa and the Yeagers. Mick and Linda walked to a far corner and stood deep in conversation.

Teddy Jo held the book she'd been skimming out to Heath. "This is a good book on soccer."

"Thanks." He glanced down at it, then back at her. "We had fun yesterday, didn't we?"

She nodded with a grin. "I'm not too good at tennis, but I want to learn. I was looking for a book on tennis."

He laughed. "I guess we both had the same idea."

Just being near him sent her pulse leaping. The book titles ran together and she couldn't read them. Her hand shook as she pulled a book out at random.

"Basketball is all right, I guess," said Heath. "Right now I'm too short to be good at it, but when I grow as tall as Mick, I'm going to play it."

Teddy Jo focused on the book she held and it was on basketball. "I'm too short to be on a team, but I know how to play." She pushed the book back in place and forced her mind to read the titles until she found a book on tennis.

"I read that one and it's good. So is this one." Heath pulled another book out and handed it to her. It didn't have as many pictures as the first, but she held it to her and nodded. Somehow she'd read every word of the book.

Heath smiled at Teddy Jo. She was pretty and

he liked her. Maybe she'd go with him if he asked her.

Across the room Mick moved nervously from one foot to the other. Why couldn't he be as relaxed with Linda as his little brother was with Teddy Jo? At fourteen he'd have been too scared to be seen with a girl, let alone talk to one.

"You don't have to talk to me if you don't want," said Linda sharply. She'd talked, but Mick had barely spoken except to tell her how Grandpa had found a tractor part for his dad's tractor.

Mick's ears turned pink. "I've been talking to you."

"I've been doing most of the talking." She flipped her long hair over her slender shoulder. She was dressed in white shorts and a peach-colored knit shirt with a scoop neck. A gold chain hung around her neck. Flat sandals were buckled to her feet and her toenails were painted the same pink as her fingernails. "Maybe I haven't given you a chance to say anything."

"I like to hear you talk." He liked the smell of her perfume and the way she looked.

She smiled. She liked to hear him talk, too. Just being with him made her feel good. She started to speak just as someone called her name. Bill Frazer walked toward her with a wide smile on his suntanned face. He wore a cotton shirt with the sleeves rolled to his elbows and faded jeans that hugged his muscular legs.

"Did you forget we have a date, Linda?"

Jealousy shot through Mick and he doubled his fists at his sides.

Linda glared at Bill. How dare he butt in when she was talking to Mick? He didn't own her just because they'd gone out several times. "I didn't forget, Bill. But it's not until tonight."

"Hey, that's right." He forced a laugh. With a surprised look he turned to Mick. "Oh, sorry, Linda. I didn't know you were talking to anyone."

"Sure, Bill." She touched Mick's arm. "Mick Yeager, Bill Frazer. Bill's going to be a senior, too, Mick."

"Do you play football?" asked Bill as if he expected the answer to be negative.

"I did in Battle Creek." Mick forced his words to be civil. He'd never felt this way before and it alarmed him.

Bill talked a few more minutes and finally walked away, telling Linda that he'd pick her up at seven.

Linda stood silently, her head down, her mind whirling. Bill wasn't really a very nice boy. What would Mick think of her now that he knew she was dating Bill?

Mick cleared his throat. "I guess I'd better go find a book before my folks want to leave."

"I guess I'd better get one, too," Linda said in a low, tight voice. She walked away and he let her go. Tears stung her eyes and she longed to run back to him and tell him that Bill meant absolutely nothing to her.

Mick turned to the bookshelf and stared unseeingly at the books. Why would Linda want to date him when she could go with a guy like Bill? He might as well forget about her. But he knew that was impossible and he stood staring at the books for a long time without moving, his heart heavy in his chest.

In the children's section Paul sat at the low table with Ty. "I heard your sister and Teddy Jo talking about King's Kids. I think we should be able to join."

Ty nodded. "Me, too. Why should we get left out just because we're not as old as they are? Can we help it that our parents didn't have us sooner?"

"I'm going to walk right up to Teddy Jo and tell her that we're going to be in the club!" Paul shook his head, but his stomach tightened alarmingly. He sure couldn't walk up to Teddy Jo and insist on anything. But he wouldn't let Ty know it. Ty probably wasn't afraid of anyone and especially not his sisters. Paul nodded. "Yes, I am! We are going to be King's Kids and that's for sure!"

Ty nodded his blond head. "We sure are!"

Across the room Teddy Jo turned to walk to the desk and bumped into Carlie. "Sorry, Carlie."

"You should be sorry!" Carlie's dark eyes flashed.

Teddy Jo blinked in surprise. "What's wrong with you?"

Carlie gripped Teddy Jo's wrist and pulled her away from Heath and down an empty aisle. She stopped and glared at Teddy Jo's surprised face.

"Hey, you said we were going to be friends, yet you spend all your time with my twin brother! I don't like that at all!"

"But you and I *are* friends. Why are you mad at me?"

Carlie tapped Teddy Jo on the chest. "I think you're in love with my brother and that's why you want to hang around with him instead of me!"

Teddy Jo's face burned. "What? How dare you say that!"

"It's true!"

"No!" Numbly Teddy Jo shook her head, then turned and ran out of the library. How could she ever face Heath again?

11. King's Kids

Teddy Jo peeked around the corner of her house.
Oh, she could not face Heath or Carlie today or
any day! How could Carlie say that she loved
Heath? Teddy Jo's cheeks burned as she thought
of the terrible confrontation in the library yesterday.

What if Carlie told Heath?

Teddy Jo sagged against the house with Happy
lying at her feet. It was too terrible to consider.
She liked Heath, really liked him, but as a friend
and not a boyfriend.

Her heart jerked. Was it possible that she liked
him for a boyfriend? She rubbed her damp
palms down her faded jeans. A cool breeze
ruffled her long hair. Would she ever be able to
face Heath again? He had planned on coming
over today. What if he did? She groaned and
peeked around the house again. Before she could
jump back out of sight Cathy and Dara saw her
and ran across the grass to her side.

"We've been looking for you, Teddy Jo." Cathy flipped a long gold braid over her slender shoulder. "Are you hiding from us?"

"She wouldn't do that," said Dara in her soft voice. "Would you, Teddy Jo?"

Teddy Jo frowned. "Why would I hide from you girls?"

Cathy leaned forward with a scowl on her face and her fists on her hips. "Because of King's Kids! That's why! You don't want us to join for some strange reason all your own and we want to know why."

Dara tugged Cathy's elbow. "Don't get mad at Teddy Jo. Let her explain why she won't let us in."

A fly landed on Teddy Jo's arm and she swatted it away. She walked to the large maple in the backyard and sank to the soft grass under it. Cathy and Dara sat cross-legged in front of her as she frantically searched her mind for something to say. No way could she be in King's Kids after what had happened yesterday!

"Start talking!" snapped Cathy.

Dara was embarrassed. She hated it when Cathy talked so angrily. Dara plucked at a piece of grass. She should've stayed at home today, but she'd wanted to learn all the information she could on the new club. It would be fun to join a club with other Christians. She might meet some boys.

Teddy Jo took a deep breath as she pulled her legs up until her knees touched her chin. She'd have to think fast. It would be terrible if the girls found out what Carlie had said to her. If they thought she loved a boy, she couldn't face them ever again. Her skin burned just thinking about it.

Happy lifted his head, barked, wagged his tail and went back to sleep with his chin on Teddy Jo's sandaled foot.

Cathy moved restlessly. King's Kids would be a lot of fun and it made her mad to think that she couldn't join. Maybe if she was around Heath long enough, he might start liking her. He might even want to go with her. She shivered and wrapped her arms around herself. Even if Heath didn't like her, he'd have his friends in the club and one of them would want to go with her. Surely someone would! She really wasn't ugly. She wasn't pretty like Dara, nor did she dress as well, but Dara was rich and had money to buy lots of clothes.

Teddy Jo locked her fingers around her knees. "I really don't think King's Kids will be that much fun. I've changed my mind about joining. If you girls are really interested, talk to Carlie."

Anger rose inside Cathy and she leaped to her feet. "You know we can't join without you! Carlie and Heath are *your* friends! They wouldn't let us in!"

Dara's face turned almost as white as her hair. "We want to be in the club, Teddy Jo! How can we if you aren't?"

Just then Carlie walked into the backyard. "Hi," she said. She looked hesitantly at Teddy Jo. Would Teddy Jo speak to her after yesterday?

Teddy Jo's face turned a brick red. She saw the pain in Carlie's brown eyes and she knew Carlie was sorry for what she'd said. But the damage was done and Teddy Jo wouldn't forgive or forget.

Cathy whirled around and smiled brightly. "Carlie! Did you come to tell us more about King's Kids?"

Carlie flushed. How could she tell them that they weren't going to start such a club? She looked helplessly at Teddy Jo, but Carlie knew even Teddy Jo thought it was for real. Carlie cleared her throat. "I suppose we could talk about it."

Teddy Jo jumped up. Her stomach was a tight, hard knot. "Not me! I have to go inside and do some homework." She ran to the back door and rushed into the warm house that smelled like tuna fish.

In the yard Carlie looked around frantically for help. Finally she had to look at the girls standing side by side, waiting for her answer. "What do you want to know?" She watched Happy run to his dog house.

"When does it start?" asked Dara.

"How many boys are in it?" asked Cathy.

Carlie wanted the ground to open up and swallow her. Lying caused a lot of trouble. She'd asked Jesus to forgive her, now she'd have to face the outcome.

"Let's go to my house since Teddy Jo had to go inside," said Cathy, motioning toward her house where Paul and Jim were playing in the backyard.

Carlie nodded and fell into step between Cathy and Dara. What would she say to the girls? Maybe it would be smart to go ahead and plan the club. She and Heath really were going to do it some day. Why not now? They could take a long time to get it organized so that they wouldn't have to start before September. By then school would be on and none of them would have much time to participate in a club.

"I know an old man who needs help with his gardening," said Dara. "We could help him as our first project."

"That's a good idea," said Cathy.

Carlie agreed. Suddenly she knew that she wanted the club to start now and not later. Her face glowed as she stopped at Cathy's back door. "We'll write down steps to starting, and set up a date to start!"

Cathy and Dara laughed happily as they walked inside.

Paul stood in the sandbox where they'd just finished building a detailed road and looked thoughtfully toward the closed door. He'd heard them talk about the club. "Jim, let's join the King's Kids."

"Cathy told me about it, but she said I was too young." Jim picked up a small blue truck. "I told her I could if I wanted to."

Paul puffed out his thin chest. "And I said I'm going to join, too! Ty Yeager's going to and that makes three of us. We should ask some of the boys in our Sunday school class. We might just get so many that we could have a club of our own!"

Jim didn't know if it would be any fun or not, but he nodded in agreement anyway.

"I just might be the president!" Paul said, puffing out his thin chest.

"I'd be the treasurer. I like to handle money." Jim's palms itched to get a hold of a pile of money right now.

Paul looked over at his yard at a movement and he saw Heath Yeager petting and talking to Happy. "Hi," called Paul as he ran toward Heath.

"Where's Teddy Jo?" Heath pushed his hands into his pockets. For some reason Teddy Jo was upset and he wanted to find her and talk to her.

"She's in the house," said Paul. "Why?"

"I want to talk to her." Heath looked toward the back door as a nervous shiver ran over him. Would she talk to him?

"Talk about what?" Paul moved from one foot to the other. Plenty of boys stopped by to talk to Linda, but none for Teddy Jo. Something was up and he wanted to know what it was.

Heath shrugged. "I just want to talk to her. I'll see you around."

Paul ran beside Heath. "Me and Jim want to be in King's Kids. Can we?"

"Ask Carlie," he said briskly. Why had Carlie started all this about King's Kids? Well, she'd have to take care of it!

Paul turned and ran back to Jim, and Heath knocked on the back door. His hand shook and he quickly stuck it behind his back. Maybe Teddy Jo wouldn't answer the door.

But she opened it, expecting to see the girls. The sight of Heath shook her so much she almost fell against the door that she held open. Her stomach fluttered and her eyes were wide in surprise.

"Can we talk, Teddy Jo?" His voice was barely above a whisper.

"Talk?"

"About what's wrong."

"What's wrong?" With a gasp she jumped back and slammed the door in his face. She pressed against it, shaking and weak.

Heath backed away from the door, a stunned look on his face. Why had she slammed the door in his face? Was she angry at him? But why would she be?

Slowly he turned and walked to the sidewalk with his head down and his shoulders drooping.

12. Lake Michigan

Teddy Jo huddled in her corner of the back seat with her arms folded and her chin on her chest. Why wouldn't Dad let her stay home today? She could not face Heath! But Dad had said that they'd agreed to have a picnic together at Lake Michigan with the Yeagers and go swimming and have an all-around fun day. Some fun! She'd have to dig a hole in the sand and bury herself!

She moved restlessly and the tie of her swim suit cut into her neck. She wore her new red suit under her blue shorts and tee shirt. Her feet were hot inside her tennis shoes. It was an hour's drive to the lake and the time was passing too quickly.

Carlie had such a big mouth! Teddy Jo doubled her fists. She would never, never forgive Carlie! A warning bell went off inside Teddy Jo. She knew that the Bible said if she didn't forgive others, God couldn't forgive her. A great sadness swept over her and tears stung her eyes. She looked out the window at the passing farmland. How could she forgive Carlie? God was asking too much of her.

But she knew she had to. Silently she asked Jesus for help and strength to forgive Carlie. She moved her mouth, but no sound came out as she said, "I forgive Carlie with Jesus' help."

Linda sat in the opposite corner with Paul in the middle, sitting on the edge of the seat so he could listen to Mom and Dad talk. With a sigh Linda looked at her pink fingernails. But her mind drifted off her appearance onto Mick. He hadn't called her since the day in the library last week. She'd broken her date with Bill, hoping Mick would call. Bill had been very angry and had said that he'd never speak to her again. She shrugged. He wasn't important to her now. Next to Mick he was nothing. Next to Mick all the other boys seemed immature and selfish.

What would she say to Mick today? Would he be cold toward her? She twisted a strand of dark hair around and around her finger. Why was it taking so long to get to Lake Michigan? Were the Yeagers and Grandma and Grandpa already there, impatiently waiting for the cook-out and swim?

What if Mick brought a girl with him?

Linda's stomach tightened and she stared out the window at the cars zooming past. What would she do if he had a girl friend? Oh, it was too horrible to consider!

Paul laughed at something Dad said and Linda studied Dad thoughtfully. He really was different now that he was a Christian. It was as if he was a new and different person. He didn't swear or drink anymore. And it had been a long time since he'd lost his temper and yelled at them. Just yesterday he'd patted the couch beside himself and asked her to sit down and talk with him. Before, he never talked to any of them, except Mom once in a while. Yes, he was different.

What would her life be like if she became a Christian?

She shook her head quickly. She wouldn't think about that today. She had enough to think about with Mick.

Mick was a Christian. Maybe he didn't want to be seen with her because she wasn't. A sob rose in her throat, but she forced it back down. Well, she wasn't good enough for him. He was pure and clean and wonderful and she wasn't. What would he see in her? Only dirt! Oh, why had she come today?

She leaned her head back dejectedly and closed her eyes and let the sounds of talking and laughing whirl around her.

At the lake Teddy Jo carried the blanket and walked beside Paul who carried the towels. Mom and Dad walked with the cooler between them and Linda lagged behind with the jug of iced tea. The sand was hot and great waves rolled up on the beach and pulled away, leaving the sand wet.

Suddenly Linda stopped, her legs weak. Just

ahead the Yeagers and Grandma and Grandpa stood around a picnic table. Mick's back was to her. A brown tank top stretched over his wide shoulders and hung down to his brown shorts. The sun turned his curls a light gold. She heard him laugh at something Grandpa said and she longed to have him turn and see her and rush to meet her with outstretched arms. But he didn't turn and she was forced to walk to the group and set the jug on the over-ladened table.

"Hi, Linda." Anna stepped forward and hugged her granddaughter warmly. "You look as beautiful as always."

Mick stood very still, his heart thudding and his stomach fluttering. She did look even more beautiful than he remembered. Would she want anything to do with him? Did she think he was a great big nothing who wasn't worth her time?

Stiffly she turned her head and her eyes locked with his. Her breath caught in her throat and all the noises around her faded into the background. He didn't act as if he hated the sight of her. A flush rose to her cheek. He actually seemed pleased to see her!

He slowly walked toward her, forcing back the shyness that threatened to ruin his day. "Hi, Linda."

"Hi." She couldn't smile or move.

"How have you been?"

"All right. You?"

"I got the summer job I wanted at the grocery store."

"I'm glad."

He could smell her perfume and he suddenly felt as if he were floating. "Shall we walk along the beach awhile?"

"I'd like that." She smiled and his heart turned over.

Side by side, without touching, they walked away from the noisy family toward the lapping waves of Lake Michigan. A red and white sailboat bobbed in the middle of the lake. The distant sound of a motorboat could be heard over the splash of the waves and the shouts of the swimmers.

At the picnic table Teddy Jo slipped her hand in Grandpa's arm and looked up into his dear face. The breeze blew his gray hair, uncovering the bald spot that never seemed to grow any bigger. She wanted him to pull her close and hold her tight the way he usually did, but she knew he was busy with the others. She knew Heath was at the end of the table, holding a red Frisbee, but she wouldn't look his way and she hoped that he wasn't looking at her.

Grandpa leaned down and said for her ears alone, "Shall we go for a walk just the two of us?"

"Please," she whispered through a tight throat.

He caught her hand in his large, work-roughened hand and they strolled along the sand down the beach away from the swimming area. Seagulls cried out, diving and dipping.

"All right, Teddy Bear Jo, what's bothering my favorite little girl?"

Tears sparkled in her blue eyes as she looked up at him. "Something is really wrong, Grandpa."

"Tell me and I'll help all I can." He squeezed her hand and she was able to smile.

Teddy Jo took a deep breath. "It's . . . it's Heath Yeager. I like him, Grandpa. I like him a lot and he's fun to be with. Carlie says I love him! Love, Grandpa! I'm not like Linda. I don't fall in love!"

Grandpa stopped at a deserted bench and sat down, tugging Teddy Jo down beside him. "Teddy Jo, you're going to be thirteen years old in just a few days. You're growing up and that's great. It really is all right to enjoy being around Heath. It's all right to love Heath, even to be in love with him. That's all part of growing up. You won't be like Linda because you're you. Don't be ashamed to be in love and to enjoy being with Heath. You two can have fun together. And you can have fun with Carlie and your other girl friends. You see, it's all right."

"But what if he finds out how I feel about him, Grandpa?" She plucked at his sleeve, her cheeks flaming.

"I think he'd be glad. Never be ashamed to love someone. God created us to love others."

She was quiet several seconds. "Grandpa, I slammed the door in his face." She quickly told him what Carlie had said and what she'd done when Heath came to visit her. "I can't talk to him again!"

Grandpa pushed her hair away from her face and gently kissed her cheek. "You can, Teddy Jo.

Remember what I told you about the words you speak?"

She nodded.

"When you say that you can't talk to him, those words build a wall of fear around you so that you can't talk to him. But you have God helping you. You can change your words! You *can* talk to him. And you won't be afraid! You'll walk right up to him and tell him that you're sorry for the way you acted and that you want to be friends."

She shook her head fearfully, her eyes wide.

Grandpa laughed softly and pulled her close and held her. She could smell his after-shave lotion and the breath mint that he sucked.

"You aren't alone, Teddy Jo. You have Jesus to help you, to give you strength. You can do it!"

Finally she nodded and smiled. "I'd better do it now before it's too late. Or before I back out." She laughed and rubbed her forehead on Grandpa's bare forearm that was tanned almost as dark as the bark on his precious black walnut trees on his property.

"You won't back out! I know you won't. You'll walk right up to him with your head high and your beautiful eyes sparkling."

His words warmed her totally. Were her eyes beautiful? Would Heath think so?

Did she love him?

The silent question took her breath away and she sat beside Grandpa without moving for a long time.

13. A New Linda

Teddy Jo stood hesitantly in the warm sand and looked toward her family and the Yeagers. Could she walk up to Heath and talk to him and tell him she was sorry? She groaned, then nodded. She could do it and she would do it!

Just then Carlie turned and saw her. Carlie took a deep breath and ran to Teddy Jo's side. "I don't want you to be mad at me, Teddy Jo."

Teddy Jo smiled and the smile came from her heart. "I'm not mad anymore, Carlie. I was really upset by what you said about Heath and me. I like him a lot and I like to be around him, but I like you, too. We can be friends even if Heath and I are friends, can't we?"

"Yes!" Carlie sighed in relief as she retied the tails of her blouse around her slender waist. "You didn't tell anyone about us begging while you were mad, did you?"

"No. I didn't tell anyone." Teddy Jo twisted her

toe in the sand. "I didn't even think about doing that." She grinned mischievously. "But it sure would've been a good way to get even."

Carlie laughed and her face turned pink with embarrassment. "I didn't think you'd tell, but somehow Dad found out." Carlie shuddered just thinking of that terrible moment. "He demanded that we explain ourselves and when Heath said that we had only wanted to help make money, he said that we could've found a better way to help. He made us give back the money to the people that we could remember. So, I have to give money back to you."

"Forget it, Carlie. It doesn't matter."

"Yes, it does! And besides, we aren't poor!" She rolled her eyes. "Heath and I are so dumb! We thought we were poor, but Dad said that we aren't. Our money is invested in the farm so we don't have much to spend right now, but it'll come."

"I'm glad you're not poor."

"It was nice of you to want to help us." Carlie looked toward the lake. Heath stood with his back to them and his head down. "I think you should talk to Heath, Teddy Jo. He thinks you hate him."

"Did you tell him what you said?" Teddy Jo held her breath.

Carlie nodded. "I'm sorry."

Teddy Jo's face flamed. "Oh, I wish you hadn't! What must he think of me?"

"I think he likes you a lot," said Carlie in a low voice as she looked at her twin.

Teddy Jo wanted so much to believe her! "Do you think so? Really think so?"

"I do."

Teddy Jo swallowed hard as she looked at Heath with the waves washing over his feet. He wore black swim trunks and a white terry shirt. "I think I will go talk to him." It took almost all the courage she had just to say that, but she lifted her head and walked away from Carlie toward the lake and Heath.

She stopped beside him, and he turned his head and his dark eyes widened in surprise. "Hi," she said softly.

"Hi." He watched her face and eyes to try to figure out what she was thinking and feeling. If she turned and walked away he didn't know what he'd do.

She bit the inside of her bottom lip and sucked in her breath. "Heath, I'm sorry for slamming the door in your face."

His eyes lit up. "You are?"

"Yes. And I'm sorry for running away from you. I was embarrassed and hurt and scared." She swallowed hard. "You see, I like you a lot and I've never liked a boy before."

He grinned from ear to ear. He wanted to leap high into the air and do flips, but he stood very still. "I like you a lot, Teddy Jo. I like being with you and doing things with you."

"You do?" Her heart almost leaped through her shirt.

Several yards down the beach Linda and Mick

walked side by side, talking about unimportant things.

Suddenly Mick stopped and faced her and she lifted her chin and watched him thoughtfully with wide blue eyes. An overwhelming desire to talk to her about God swept over him. He had prayed daily for her and he wanted her to know God in a personal way.

"Linda, God loves you."

"What?" Her heart raced alarmingly.

"He does! He created all of this for you to enjoy!" Mick told her how God had created Adam, and that Adam had sinned, bringing about a separation between God and man. "God loves man and he wanted to find a way to have fellowship with him again. He sent Jesus to earth to live as a man and die on the cross to pay the penalty we deserve for our sins. After Jesus died, he was buried. But he didn't stay in that grave!"

Linda listened as if she'd never heard this before. And it seemed as if she hadn't. It suddenly all made sense to her.

Mick caught Linda's hands and held them firmly. "Jesus came back to life and conquered death! He talked and walked with the disciples and then one day he was caught up in a cloud and taken into heaven where he is still alive!" Mick smiled into Linda's eyes. "Jesus did that for you, for me. He's already saved you from destruction, from hell, but unless you accept what he offers, it won't help you. You have to make the decision. You have to receive him as the Lord of your life and tell others that you have. He loves you, Linda, just as much as he loves me and everyone else."

Tears filled her eyes and slipped down her rosy cheeks. "I don't know if I'm ready, Mick."

"You're ready, Linda. You know there is a great loneliness inside you that is always there and you're tired of it. That loneliness is caused by not having fellowship with God the way he created you. He loves you. He wants you to talk with him. He wants to guide your life, Linda, so that you will have the very best life possible."

Her heart raced and she couldn't stop the gush of tears. "I do want Jesus," she whispered brokenly.

Tears stung Mick's eyes and a great happiness rose inside him. "I'll pray with you."

"Please do." She bowed her head and waited for him to begin.

Mick's heart leaped with joy. "Lord Jesus, Linda wants you to be her Lord and Savior. She is giving her life to you so that in its place you can give her a new spirit, a spirit made in God's image."

When Mick finished praying Linda haltingly prayed. When she lifted her head she knew that just like the others in her family, she was a new creature in Christ. She was not the same Linda, but a new one. She dashed away her tears and smiled happily. "This is the best day of my life, Mick."

"It's one of the best in mine." He gave her a

hug, then stepped back but kept his hands on her shoulders. "Now, the next step is to get to know your new Father. God is your heavenly Father. He knows you and he wants you to know him."

Linda listened happily as Mick explained to her that it was vital to read her Bible, go to church, and be around other Christians.

"God has an enemy and that is Satan," said Mick. "Jesus already took away Satan's power and authority, but Satan tries to fool people into thinking differently. He is out to destroy everyone, even you. The Bible says if you resist him he has to flee. When he gives you a thought and tries to make you think this business of being a Christian is of no importance, you tell him to leave you alone in Jesus' name and he'll have to take the thought and leave. Just learn about God and how he wants you to live by reading the Bible and praying. All of God's power is available to you to fight the enemy."

Mick took her hand again and they strolled along the beach. "Just remember God is in you and he is greater than Satan! And I'll always be around to help you."

"Thank you, Mick. Grandpa has been praying for our family for years now. Finally our whole family knows God! They'll love it when I tell them that I'm a Christian now!"

Mick caught her close and swung her around with a loud whoop. "I am so happy!"

Several minutes later they walked toward the family, talking and laughing and enjoying just being together. Linda spotted Grandpa as he stepped away from the others and turned toward them. A great love for him welled up inside her until she thought she would burst.

"I want to tell Grandpa right now, Mick."

"Go ahead." Mick watched as she flew over the sand to Ed. Her long hair waved out behind her and Mick smiled.

Linda caught Grandpa and hugged him tightly.

"What's up, Linda?" he asked with a laugh as he held her.

She lifted her face. "Grandpa, I am a Christian! Mick and I prayed and I gave myself to Jesus!"

Tears filled his hazel eyes. "Praise the Lord!" He held her close and she pressed her face into his neck and wept for joy.

14. Happy Birthday, Teddy Jo

Teddy Jo walked listlessly toward Greer Park. Today was her thirteenth birthday and no one had remembered. Grandpa had said that he'd meet her in the park at noon, but he hadn't said a word about her birthday.

She blinked back hot tears. She'd asked Heath to do something special with her today because of her birthday, but he had had plans that he couldn't or wouldn't break.

"Teddy Jo! Wait for me!"

She turned in surprise to see Linda running toward her. What a change in Linda since she'd become a Christian! Teddy Jo grinned. There had been a gigantic change in herself, too. She didn't feel like the same girl and probably Linda didn't either.

"Happy birthday, Teddy Jo."

"You remembered!"

"Of course. How could I forget my favorite

sister's birthday?" The words surprised Linda as much as they did Teddy Jo. "You know, Teddy Jo, I do love you! For a long time I hated everyone in our family."

"Me, too."

"But not any longer! I feel like I could hug the whole world!" Linda twirled around, her long hair swinging out from her slender body.

"I thought you had a date with Mick."

"I do." Linda smiled dreamily. "He's wonderful!" She turned to Teddy Jo. "You like Heath a lot, don't you?"

Teddy Jo nodded self-consciously.

"Just don't do like I did and fall for every boy that comes along. Heath's a nice boy. Stick with him."

Teddy Jo smiled. "I will."

Linda talked with Teddy Jo all the way to the wishing well in the park. Suddenly she stopped talking in mid-sentence and Teddy Jo saw her look beyond her. Teddy Jo turned to see who Linda was looking at.

"SURPRISE!"

Teddy Jo looked at her family, the Yeager family, and several friends. She gulped and stumbled back a step.

"Happy birthday, Teddy Jo!" shouted Paul.

Grandpa started singing "Happy Birthday" to her and everyone joined in. Teddy Jo stood in shock. Could this really be happening to her?

Heath stepped forward. "Come with me, Teddy Jo."

In a daze she walked around a clump of bushes with him and saw a gigantic birthday cake, decorated in yellow and white with thirteen yellow candles on it. Three picnic tables were pushed together end to end with a long white paper covering over them. Vases of yellow and white daises stood at the center of each table and a bunch of yellow and white balloons floated on their strings hooked to the end of the table.

"It's a surprise," said Paul, grinning happily. Maybe they'd give him a surprise birthday party just like this when he was thirteen. He dashed to the table and around it to stand with Ty. Just yesterday the King's Kids had met for the first time and agreed to let Ty, Paul, and Jim enter. Today was a double celebration.

Heath tugged Teddy Jo's hand. "Now, look over here." He led her to a table decorated with daisies and balloons. Gifts wrapped in bright colors sat on the table and Teddy Jo stared at them with her mouth open.

"Are they for me?"

"All for you," said Grandpa with a wink.

"A girl only has one thirteenth birthday," said Dad. He pulled Teddy Jo close and she wrapped her arms around him and hugged him hard. Since he'd become a Christian he'd learned to love her. Tears filled her eyes and she quickly blinked them away as she stepped back from him.

"Happy birthday, honey," said Mom, hugging Teddy Jo.

"Who planned this?" asked Teddy Jo, looking

117

around in awe. She remembered her eleventh birthday party that she and Cathy had planned together. But this one had been a complete surprise.

"Dad and I planned it," said Carol with a pleased smile. "We had fun doing it, didn't we, Larry?"

"We sure did." Larry nodded with a grin. "But I wouldn't want to do it every day."

"Let's eat now," said Carol. "And then we'll have cake and ice cream."

Teddy Jo watched as everyone worked together to put out fried chicken, potato salad, carrot sticks with vegetable dip, relishes of all kinds, sweet smelling rolls, and Jell-O salads that made her mouth water.

Talking and laughing filled the air. Linda smiled up at Mick and he caught her hand and squeezed it. "Isn't this wonderful, Mick? I'm so happy for Teddy Jo." Just a few days ago she knew she'd have stood here green with envy and jealousy. But no longer!

Mick slipped his arm around Linda's waist. "Just having you beside me is wonderful!" It was great to be over his shyness with her.

"I love you," she whispered with tears in her wide blue eyes.

He leaned down until he was almost touching his lips to hers. "I love you."

Much later Teddy Jo stood alone and watched her friends and family. It was hard to believe all the wonderful gifts she'd received. The cake had been delicious as well as beautiful. She touched a yellow candle that she'd slipped into her pocket. It was her souvenir of this fantastic thirteenth birthday. She'd keep it always.

Cathy ran to Teddy Jo's side. "I'm glad your mom invited me. It's so exciting!"

"I can't believe it's happening to me."

"Do you think you'll be able to come to King's Kids Monday morning? I know you have reading class."

"Friday was my last day." She stood straighter. The teacher had said she'd improved an entire grade level this summer, and that if she kept working at it, she'd soon be reading seventh grade level. It was a miracle from God!

"Good, then we'll see you at Dara's house Monday at ten."

"She makes a good president, doesn't she?"

Cathy nodded. "And Carlie's a good treasurer. Heath seems happy to be vice-president." Cathy narrowed her eyes thoughtfully. Someday she'd be president and she'd make the best one ever!

"I'm going to see what Carlie wants." Teddy Jo saw Carlie motioning urgently for her. "Thanks for the necklace, Cathy."

"I'm glad you like it. Maybe I can borrow it sometime."

Teddy Jo laughed and nodded as she ran to Carlie's side. "Why are you dancing around, Carlie? What's made you so excited?"

"Look! Look over there!" She pointed to several boys playing Frisbee tag. "See the one with black hair and a red tee shirt?"

"I see him. That's Joe Boleen."

"He talked to me! The Frisbee flew over here and I caught it and gave it back to him and he talked to me! I think I'm in love." Carlie pressed her hand to her heart and sighed.

Teddy Jo laughed. "I'll introduce you to him when he's done playing. He's a Christian. We'll see if he wants to be in the King's Kids."

"Oh, I'm going to convince him he wants to join!"

Teddy Jo walked away from Carlie toward Grandpa. He winked at her and she smiled. "All this is too great for words, Grandpa!"

"I know." He looked at his family, then turned back to Teddy Jo. "Remember just three years ago when no one was a Christian in the Miller family?"

"I remember and it was awful!"

"Now, all the Larry Miller family are part of God's family! This is a happy day, Teddy Jo. Our prayers have been answered."

"We seem like a different family. It's funny, isn't it?"

"It's fantastic!" He hugged her close and she felt his whiskers rub against her soft cheek. "I love you, Teddy Bear Jo."

"I love you, Grandpa!"

Just then Ely Yeager called to Grandpa and he

walked away, looking as tall and strong as the large oak that shaded the picnic tables.

Heath saw Teddy Jo standing alone and he smiled as he walked toward her. She liked him! His heart leaped and he wanted to jump for joy.

Teddy Jo saw him walking toward her and she smiled. He didn't look at all like the ragged beggar that he once had been. The sun turned his curls into a bright halo around his head. He smiled at her and suddenly she knew. She loved him! She did! She hid a smile behind her hand and tried to dim the sparkle in her bright blue eyes. She loved him!

"Hi, Teddy Jo."

"Hi." Excitement bubbled up inside her.

"How about a game of soccer?"

"I'd love it!"

"Dad bought me a soccer ball since he said I was determined to play it. Let's go get it from the car."

She ran across the grass toward the car with Heath at her side.

She loved him!

Someday she'd tell him. Maybe.

If you enjoyed the Teddy Jo series,
read the exciting adventures of Elizabeth Gail!

If you enjoyed the Teddy Jo series,
double your fun with the Tyler Twins!

The Tyler Twins series is available at your local bookstore, or you may order by mail (U.S. and territories only). Send your check or money order plus $.75 per book ordered for postage and handling to:

Tyndale D.M.S.
Box 80
Wheaton, IL 60189

Prices subject to change.
Allow 4-6 weeks for delivery.

Tyndale House Publishers, Inc.